The Flame of Fire House

MICHELLE JARVIS

PAPER MAGE PUBLISHING

From a little spark may burst a flame.

— DANTE ALIGHIERI

Contents

One

Rosalinde wrapped her cloak tighter around her as she stood on the platform outside the Air house spire, her mind still whirling from the recent encounter with Graeme. She had narrowly escaped, but the weight of abandoning those imprisoned in Air house hung heavy on her shoulders. The frigid gusts blew by her, a stark contrast to the fiery turmoil brewing inside.

Tancred, clad in an oversized coat that hung loose on his recently thin shoulders, motioned for Ros to follow him. "We have to hurry. Graeme will surely muster a party to fight, and we don't want to be caught out here when the storm hits." He nodded at Cordelia and said, "We need to get her to safety. Somewhere I can heal her."

"Fire house," Cordelia said. With a whisper, she added, "Home."

Ros nodded, her resolve hardening. They had to reach Fire house and find a way to set things right, but they couldn't go running in without a plan. Not with every-thing that had happened and all the things she had learned. Now that she had rescued her father, it was time to reclaim her place in this fractured kingdom. As her thoughts whirled within her mind, the wind howled louder around them.

Cassian's hand gripping her arm pulled her attention back to where they were, and the breeze died down in response. "It's you," he said. "You're controlling the wind."

Ros met his gaze. "There's a storm coming in."

"*You* are the storm," he said.

The bridge they'd crossed swayed dangerously under the relentless gusts. Ros took a deep breath, focusing on the steadfast way Cassian stood beside her, grounded her. Each intake of breath let the air around them fall away. She couldn't afford to let fear and anger slow her down or endanger those around her.

"Let's get out of here," she said once the risk of a storm had passed.

"I can shadow-walk us," Cassian said, "but not into Fire house. There are wards, not to mention the guards. We may be returning the lost le Fevre daughter, but before we can reap that reward, we'll need to convince them we aren't responsible for taking her."

"Get us somewhere safe where we can regroup. We'll figure out the rest after we get some rest," Ros said.

Cassian moved his grip to Rosalinde's hand. With her other hand, she grabbed hold of her father. With a nod of consent, Cordelia allowed Cassian to put his arm around her waist so that she could lean her weight on him. He said, "Hold on," and within the span of a blink, they were gone.

OMBRETTA'S COTTAGE was dark and foreboding as they appeared in front of it. Ros saw the expression on Cassian's face change when he took in the look of the place, and the fear that crossed his features the longer they stood there without Ombretta coming out to greet them.

Guilt flooded Ros for not already telling Cassian about his mother's departure and his own heritage. He was part Fae, his family from a completely different world, and he had no idea. It should have been the first thing she said when she saw him, but she'd been so caught up in everything else that was happening, in everything she had to do, she had all but forgotten.

"Cas," she said, the confession sitting on her lips.

"Just a moment," he said. "Something's wrong."

"I know. About your mother—"

Cassian put a hand up to stop her, but Ros saw the crease of his brow, the way he gave her a wary look even as he pushed through the gate, marched up the flagstones, and entered the round doorway into the cottage. She heard him calling out for his mother, the pitch of his voice edged with tightly controlled panic. Ros felt terrible for him, especially knowing she could have prevented this before it started.

When he appeared in the doorway again, Ros stepped forward and put her hands on his shoulders. "She's gone."

"Where?"

"Faerie," Ros said matter-of-factly.

Confusion, shock, and fear passed over his face before he schooled his expression into something controlled. "Why?"

"We should sit down," Ros said, "and have a proper conversation about this. You might want some privacy to —"

"Tell me."

Ros swallowed, aware that King Tancred and the Lady le Fevre were listening to every word she uttered. She could trust her father, but Ros did not know what his reaction would be to this news. And with Cordelia, she hadn't a clue how the woman would react or what she might do with the knowledge.

"Ombretta is from Faerie. Her brothers still live there. She returned to help them fight against an evil that has taken over their home."

Cassian's jaw clenched and his words came out clipped as he said, "And what about the evil taking over *our* home? The same evil she helped create."

"She had to go," Ros said. "Your mother is their only hope."

"Are we going to glide over the fact that you're Fae?" Cordelia asked.

Cassian's face hardened. "I'm not denying or ignoring it; I didn't know."

Ros could see the conflict in his eyes, the weight of everything crashing down on him. She squeezed his hand gently. "It will take time to sort out, so you shouldn't feel obligated to have answers tonight—for us or yourself. We all have parts of ourselves we're still discovering. It doesn't change who you are, Cassian."

He nodded, his expression softening slightly as he looked at her. "What now?"

Ros took a deep breath. "We should regroup and plan our next move. Ombretta may be gone, but her cottage is still a haven for us."

King Tancred, who had been silent, finally spoke. "We need to get Cordelia inside. She needs rest, and we should figure out how to get her to Fire house safely."

Cassian stepped aside, allowing Ros and her father to lead Cordelia into the cottage. Inside, it was as dark and foreboding as it had appeared from the outside, but Ros felt a sense of familiarity and comfort. Ombretta's presence remained through every aspect of the cozy dwelling, even in her absence.

They settled Cordelia on a worn but comfortable couch near the hearth. King Tancred immediately set about starting a fire, the flickering flames casting long shadows on the walls.

Ros turned to Cassian, who was still standing in the doorframe, looking lost. "We'll figure this out," she breathed. "We're in this together."

He nodded, finally stepping fully into the room and closing the door behind him. "What's the plan?"

Ros glanced at her father, who was now sitting next to Cordelia, gently checking her wounds. "First, we need to make sure Cordelia is stable. Outwardly, she's weak, but mostly seems fine. But inwardly..."

Cassian said, "Fortunately, we have your father with us, and he's widely regarded as one of the greatest Healers of all time."

"He is, but I don't know if he can fix what has happened to her."

"Maybe someone else can," Cassian said, confidence pouring out through his words and building Rosalinde's faith that they could make it somehow.

She nodded. "We'll need to figure out how to approach Fire house without getting ourselves captured. And find a way around the fire moat."

Cassian frowned. "That's a tall order. The wards are strong, and the guards will be on high alert after all that's been happening in the kingdom."

"I know," Ros said. "But we don't have a choice. Fire house is the only place where we can find the resources and allies we need to stand against Graeme, Gaius, and their forces."

King Tancred looked up from his work. "We'll need a distraction," he said thoughtfully. "Something to draw their attention away from the entrance long enough for us to get inside."

Ros nodded. "And we'll need to convince them we're not a threat. Cordelia's presence will help, but we need to be prepared for resistance."

Cassian ran a hand over his head, frustration evident in his expression. "I wish I could help more. If only I could shadow-walk us directly inside..."

Ros placed a hand on his arm. "You're doing everything you can. We'll find a way."

The fire crackled in the hearth, casting a warm glow over the room. Despite the challenges ahead, Ros felt a sense of determination settling over her. They had come this far, and they wouldn't give up now.

"We'll rest here for the night," she said. "In the morning, we'll come up with a plan to get into Fire house. Cordelia will be able to help once she's rested. We can do this. Together."

Cassian nodded, and for the first time since they had arrived, a small smile tugged at the corner of his mouth. "Together," he echoed.

Two

The next morning dawned clear and cold, and as Ros stood in the garden, she breathed in the crisp air filled with the scent of pine and earth. Ros had been the first to rise; slipping quietly out of her makeshift bed, she had wandered out into the flowers to clear her head. There was so much to sort through, and the starting place was muddy at best. But here she could stand in the calmness of nature and let her hammering heart settle into something more solid. She would need to be unshakeable if she was going to fix Talabrih and return peace to the throne.

Ros headed to the small kitchen area and set about preparing a simple breakfast, her mind already working on their plan for the day. One by one, the others stirred. Cassian joined her in the kitchen, his expression more resolved than it had been the night before. King Tancred helped Cordelia to a chair near the table, her face pale but determined.

"We need to approach Fire house cautiously," Ros began as they gathered around the table. "We'll travel through the forest to avoid detection and find a vantage point where we can observe the guards, the moat, and the wards."

Cassian nodded. "I can shadow-walk to scout ahead, look for the best route until we get close to their perimeter. Move quickly, but carefully."

King Tancred leaned forward, his eyes focused. "Once we're close, we'll need to do something that will draw the guards away so we can slip inside."

Cordelia spoke up, her voice weak but steady. "I can help with that. I may not be at full strength, but having the lost daughter of Fire house return should make for an easy distraction."

Ros looked at Cordelia, concern clear in her eyes. "Are you sure you're up for this?"

Cordelia nodded. "I have to be. This is our best chance to get you inside. And we need to make it happen if we're going to fight Graeme. I won't let him get away with what he did to me, what he's done to so many others."

"We're ignoring the most obvious solution," Cas said. "We walk to the front gate at your side, allow the guards to take us inside, and you explain to your father what really happened."

Ros shook her head. "I'm wanted as a traitor to the

crown. The moment the Lord Ruler of Fire house sees me, he is required to turn me over."

"You could claim asylum," Cassian said.

"Gilthroy is loyal to the throne and whoever occupies it," Tancred said. "He will honor the law."

Rosalinde's brows furrowed as an idea took shape. Slowly, she said, "But you aren't a wanted man; if anything, they would be heroes for finding the lost king. And you have always been friendly with Lord le Fevre. A call for protection might work if you show up with his daughter, since you only stopped being the king when you were forcibly removed."

Cassian, Tancred, and Ros turned their gazes to Cordelia. After a moment, she nodded and said, "It could work. Father always spoke favorably of you, King Tancred, and hoped to bond our houses together. The return of the true ruler of Talabrih through the might of Fire house would be a boon for him, especially if he could gain a future favor from it."

Her words were not lost on Ros. Florian had been a frontrunner for her hand, and had things gone differently at the Great Match, she may have ended up as his wife.

Ros looked up to find her father's eyes moving between her and Cassian. A smile curled the corners of his lips, and he turned back to Cordelia, saying, "I will be in your father's debt for years to come, but Princess Rosalinde is already spoken for."

"I'm certain he'll find another solution," she said. "My

father is a wise and cunning friend to those who keep their promises."

"It's settled. Cordelia and I will go to the gates and sort things out with Lord le Fevre, while you and our Night companion will look for allies elsewhere."

With the plan set, they finished their breakfast and prepared to leave. With Rosalinde's insistence, they each took a blade from the Night house cache; though Cassian was skilled with the sword, Tancred hadn't trained for years, and both women were accustomed to relying on their magic to get them out of trouble. It didn't matter. There was a nagging feeling in the back of Rosalinde's mind to make sure all of them were armed with a weapon, and she wouldn't let it go. Her father chose a short sword, and Cordelia strapped a pair of knives at her waist. Rosalinde found a bandolier that belonged to Cassian's mother, and as she dressed in Ombretta's pants, tunic, and boots, she equipped the belt with its eight sharp knives.

Cassian was able to shadow-walk them to a few familiar points on the journey and kept them out of the danger of being recognized when they were close to villages, but eventually he ran out of waypoints and they had to walk. Even then, Cassian led the way, his keen eyes scanning the forest as they moved through the trees.

As they traveled, the wilderness around them grew denser, trees towering above them and casting long shadows on the ground. The air was filled with the sounds of birds and rustling leaves, a clear contradiction to the tension that hung over their small group.

They had been traveling for several hours without a break when Cassian suddenly stopped, holding up a hand to signal the others to halt. Ros moved up beside him, her heart pounding.

"What is it?" she whispered.

Cassian pointed ahead, where a group of figures moved through the trees. "Bandits."

Ros glanced back at the others, her mind racing. They couldn't afford to be delayed or harmed by the rogues, not when they were so close to Fire house. She took a deep breath, steeling herself for what was to come.

"Let's try to avoid them," she said. "We'll go around and stay out of sight."

But as they moved, a twig snapped underfoot, and the thieves' heads turned in their direction. A shout went up, and within moments, the bandits were upon them.

Cassian moved quickly, stepping in front of Ros and Cordelia. Ros sidestepped his protection and raised her hands, ready to fight.

"Stay behind me," Cassian said, his voice calm but firm.

"I can help," she said. "I will not continue running from danger while you stand before me."

"Rosalinde, this isn't the time to be brave."

"I could say the same to you. You need to learn to accept my help, even if you don't like it."

The bandits closed in, their faces twisted with malice. The leader, a tall man with a scar running down his cheek, stepped forward, his eyes twinkling with a mix of amusement and interest.

"Well, well, what have we here?" he drawled, his smooth and melodic voice a direct contradiction to his dangerous appearance. "Looks like we've interrupted a lovers' spat, boys."

The bandits laughed, but Cassian said, "We don't want any trouble. Let us pass, and we'll be on our way."

"Don't know that we can do that," the leader said. "I'm rightly curious about what has that lovely lady of yours up in arms."

"That's between us," Cas said through gritted teeth.

The man's brows knit together. "Not a very kind way of introducing yourselves. A group of travelers wandering into our territory? Normally I'd have you hand over your valuables, and we might let you live. But here you are, being a right twat about this robbery."

"I want to fight you," Ros said, her voice shakier than she liked. "But he wants to give in and stay out of trouble. That's what we're arguing about."

The bandit leader laughed, a rich, warm sound that didn't quite match the situation. His storm-gray eyes twinkled with mischief. "Trouble? No, no, you've got it all wrong. I'm a businessman, you see. And business is good when you have the right merchandise." He winked at Ros.

Cassian stepped forward. "We're not here to make deals. Let us pass, or you'll regret it."

The leader raised one black eyebrow, a smirk playing on his lips. "What happened to not wanting trouble?"

"Sense has finally returned to his addled brain," Ros said.

"Feisty, aren't you? I like that. Name's Darian, by the way. And who might you be?"

Cassian's eyes narrowed. "Not interested in pleasantries."

Darian sighed dramatically, shaking his head. "Always so serious. Alright, how about this: you give us something shiny, and we let you go. Fair?"

Ros looked pointedly at Cassian for a moment before turning back at Darian. "We have nothing to give you. We're on an urgent mission."

Darian's expression softened slightly, a glimmer of genuine curiosity in his eyes. "A mission, huh? Well, now I'm intrigued. What kind of mission brings such a colorful group through these dangerous woods?"

King Tancred stepped forward, his voice steady. "We're trying to save our kingdom. Please, let us pass. We have no quarrel with you."

Darian studied them for a moment, his playful demeanor slipping. "Saving a kingdom, you say? That's quite the undertaking." He glanced at his men, then back at the group. "Alright, you've piqued my interest. But I still need to make a living, you know."

Before anyone could react, Cassian drew his sword. He was a vortex of movement, his weapon flashing in the morning light as he engaged the bandits. Ros felt the bracelet Ombretta had given her burning against her skin, and fire burst at her fingertips as she prepared to join the fray.

Darian, instead of joining the fight, watched with a mixture of admiration and exasperation. "Elementalists? Fascinating. But we could have talked this out, you know."

Cassian was a whirlwind of power and grace, his Fae heritage giving him an edge in speed and strength, even if he hadn't known that was where his enhanced skills came from. As the fight continued and several of Darian's people were injured, the bandit leader finally drew his own sword, a gleaming weapon that looked almost out of place in his hands. He moved with surprising skill, parrying Cassian's strikes with ease.

"You're good," Cassian admitted through gritted teeth.

Darian grinned. "You're not so bad yourself. Shame we couldn't have met under different circumstances."

Despite the ferocity of the bandits, they weren't willing to engage Ros once they saw the power at her fingertips. She didn't even have to draw her blades. Several backed away, making a path between her and the fight with Cassian and their leader. She made her way toward Darian, her eyes locked on his.

"Stand down, Darian!" she shouted. "We don't want to hurt you."

Darian laughed. A strand of his hair came loose from the tie holding it back, and it curled along his jaw as he gave Ros a lazy smile. "Too late for that, princess. But I do admire your spirit."

Princess, she thought. *So, he knew exactly who he was robbing.*

With a final, desperate swing, Darian lunged at Cassian, but Cassian was quicker. His sword found its mark, and Darian crumpled to the ground, clutching his side.

Breathing heavily, Ros looked around at the aftermath. The bandits lay scattered on the forest floor, and their group was bloodied but victorious. She turned to Cassian, who was wiping his sword clean.

"Are you alright?" she asked, her voice trembling slightly.

Cassian nodded, his expression grim. "We're fine. But we need to move. The noise might attract more trouble."

Ros agreed. They prepared to leave, but before they could move, Darian's voice called out weakly. "Wait... I wasn't lying. I can help you."

Ros turned back, her eyes narrowing. "Why should we trust you?"

Darian managed a weak smile. "Because I know these woods better than anyone. And because... well, let's just say I have my reasons for wanting to see your family remain on the throne."

Cassian and Ros exchanged a look. Despite everything, there was something in Darian's eyes that spoke of sincerity. Ros sheathed her sword and stepped forward, offering him a hand.

"Alright, Darian," she said. "You can come with us."

Darian pointed at Tancred. "No offense, but I'd rather take his hand, and a bit of healing with it, if you don't mind." He moved his hand from his side to show blood blooming through his shirt.

Tancred moved to his side and worked for only a moment. The blood ceased and his side stitched itself up at Tancred's touch.

Ros said, "If you betray us..."

The bandit stood with a wince. "I won't. You have my word. Whatever that's worth."

"Not much," Cassian muttered.

"I'll prove my worth to you."

Ros sighed. "I guess we'll find out, won't we?"

Three

As they moved farther into the woods that protected Fire house, the forest grew dense and dark, the canopy above blocking out much of the fading light. The tree trunks here were narrower than those in the land surrounding Water house but they grew closer together, making the area far more difficult to navigate. Ros, Cassian, King Tancred, and Cordelia followed Darian closely as he led them through the winding paths and hidden trails. Ros was certain they would have gotten lost without their bandit guide. Darian moved with confidence, his eyes sharp and alert, his every step sure and purposeful.

"We need to keep moving," Darian said, his voice low. "These woods are full of dangers, and the outlaws you encountered earlier are simply one of many threats."

As if on cue, the forest seemed to close in around them, the breeze thick with the scent of sap and damp earth. The sounds of nocturnal creatures emerging into the night filled the air, their calls echoing through the trees.

"The bandits we encountered?" Ros asked, brows going high. "Those were *your* men."

Darian waved his hand dismissively. "A collection of unlucky gits and unlikely allies. You know what that's like, Princess?"

Ros bit the inside of her cheek. He wasn't wrong. Ros had found herself in the company of several people she would've never imagined prior to finding them in her path at the right time. "Suppose I do. I've allied myself with you, after all. At least for the time being."

Darian laughed, and Ros was struck yet again with how full and lovely it sounded. "That you are, to your great fortune. As you've surely noticed by now, I'm an absolute delight."

Ros glanced at Cassian, whose expression said that he disagreed with the bandit wholeheartedly.

All at once, Darian held up a hand to signal them to stop. "The Deuil River is ahead," he whispered. "We'll need to cross it, but it's not safe. There are things in the water that can sense our presence."

"What sort of things?" Cas asked.

"Water wraiths," Darian replied. "Beings who have died in the crossing, drowned by the water that still holds them captive. They're drawn to the living, craving what they've lost."

"I've never heard of such a thing," Ros said.

"Of course not," Darian said. "What would a princess know of the dangers in the wild?"

"I've crossed this river dozens of times over the years and no one has mentioned these creatures."

Darian shook his head. "Have you crossed anywhere besides the royal road? Have you fled in the night, escaping a cruel lord or an arranged marriage or the violent hands of a lover?" He swallowed hard, his expression far away for a moment. Finally, he blinked away whatever held him in that distant place, and said, "No, you've never experienced those dangers, so you've never crossed the Deuil anywhere that wasn't safe. You haven't risked your life to make sure your child could be free..." he said, his voice cracking.

"You're right," Tancred said. "I have experienced none of those things. I'm sorry that any of my people have."

Darian gave a terse nod. "We'll need to cross quickly and quietly."

"Are you up for it?" Tancred asked. Though his words were meant for Cordelia, all eyes turned to them.

Cordelia's face hardened as she met their inquiring gazes. "Stop worrying over me."

"You're hurt," Tancred said.

"Hurt, not broken," she said. "I can do this."

"We don't want to risk—"

"I said I'm fine," she said, pulling herself up to her full height. She was dirty, her clothes ragged and torn, and her body and face marred from months of captivity, but in that moment she had the bearing of nobility.

Tancred nodded. "Very well, Lady le Fevre."

Darian led them to the river's edge. The group approached the Deuil cautiously, Darian's warning echoing in the backs of their minds. The water was dark and swift, the current strong. He moved to the edge of the shore and dipped his fingers into the water, swirling them around. After a moment, Darian withdrew his hand and shook the droplets from his skin. "We can't cross here."

"Why?" Cassian asked. He'd barely said anything since Darian had joined them, and his sudden question startled Ros.

Darian pointed out toward the water. "The current is wild tonight, hungry. If we pass through at this point, someone will die.

Cas rolled his eyes. "You can't know that for certain, and there's no need to be dramatic in an attempt to scare us."

"I *do* know it for certain, whether or not you choose to believe it."

Cas made to step forward into the water, but Ros put a hand on his shoulder. "We have decided to trust Darian to get us to Fire house. He says it isn't safe to cross here."

"You can't really believe him," Cassian said. "I don't know why he doesn't want us to cross here; maybe he's trying to lead us to where his accomplices are waiting to ambush us."

Darian laughed mirthlessly. "My *accomplices* are in the woods behind us. The only thing I'm trying to do is keep you lot from killing yourselves."

"Ros could use her Water magic to get us across," Cas said.

She shook her head in response. "I've already tried reaching out to the water here. I... I can't speak to it. I'm unsure why."

"As have I," Tancred said. "Though my powers are healing, water still responds when I call. But not here."

Darian gave a small nod. "I am not surprised. This place is tainted, filled with darkness and blood. It is best that you can't speak to it; you wouldn't want any part of these waters to attach to your magic."

Ros furrowed her brows at the words. Darian seemed to understand something about elemental magic that he had yet to tell them. It made Ros wonder exactly who he was, and what else he was hiding.

"Fine," Cassian said. "I'll shadow-walk us to the other side."

"The Deuil is the border of Fire house's land. Their wards prevent you from using your magic to get inside," Tancred said.

With a sigh of frustration, Cassian gave up his protests and Darian led them to a narrow part of the river where the water seemed slightly calmer. The bandit said, "We'll cross here. There are stones we can walk on for part of the way, but they disappear when we get close to the middle and we'll need to get into the water. Hold tight to one another. Step lightly and don't make any sudden movements."

They took one another's hands—Darian leading, followed by Ros, Tancred, Cordelia, and Cassian bringing up the rear—and began to cross the river single file, care-fully stepping on the stones that protruded above the water. Ros felt her heart pounding in her chest, each step bringing her closer to the opposite bank. She imagined she could see the shadowy forms of the water wraiths lurking beneath the surface, their eyes glowing faintly in the dark-ness, but when she blinked they were gone, as if they had never been there.

Darian moved steadily across the river, his movements deliberate and controlled. As they reached the halfway point, a sudden splash broke the silence. Ros turned to see Cordelia slipping on a wet stone, her foot plunged into the water. Tancred and Cassian reacted quickly, pulling her back onto the stone, but from the corner of her eye Ros was certain she saw *something* in the water nearby, watch-ing. Waiting.

"Keep going," Darian called back. "Stop for nothing!"

But they had to stop. Or slow, at the least, because the stones were no longer there to help them across.

Darian was in the water already. Despite the danger, his gaze was focused on Rosalinde. Her eyes darted around him, searching the dark waters. He reached for her, saying, "Eyes on me, Princess."

"The wraiths—"

"Just me," he said, his voice far calmer than it had a right to be. "You're going to take my hands and climb into the water."

She shook her head. "It's too deep."

"No, it's not. My feet are touching the bottom."

"You're tall."

He smiled. "Not exceptionally. You'll be fine. And you're a Water mage. Even if you can't command this river, it still knows you."

"What if—"

"Now, Princess, before you get us all killed."

There was no hesitation in his command. His words were matter-of-fact, and the truth of it sent Ros into action. She grabbed his hands and climbed down into the water. Her teeth were chattering before her feet touched the riverbed.

"Don't stop," Darian said. "One foot after another until you can climb back onto the rocks. We'll be right behind you."

Ros didn't argue. She waded through the water, chest high and going higher as she moved into the deeper part at the center of the river. She heard the splash behind her as someone else dropped into the water—her father, most likely. Ros didn't turn around to see.

She could see the rocks emerging from the water in front of her, and though it felt as if she was barely making progress, they grew ever closer with each step. Ros was nearly upon them when she felt something brush against the back of her legs.

Rosalinde's heart plummeted to her feet. *No,* she thought. *I'm so close. A few more steps...*

The water wraiths circled around her, brushing against her goose-pimpled skin. Ros tried to ignore them despite the whimper rising in her throat, but as they surged in front of her, their eyes flashing a violent shade of yellow, she could avoid them no longer. Ros called to the magic coursing through her blood. She had known the power of water for as long as she could remember, and reaching for it now was as familiar as breathing. The water answered, and though it was barely a whisper, she could hear the magic answering her call.

Before she could draw the water to do her bidding, she heard Darian yelling behind her: "Don't use the water!"

Ros didn't turn to answer him, afraid to take her eyes from the wraiths. "I can feel it. I think I can avoid the dark parts of the magic."

"No!" Darian called, his voice a knife through the air.

Ros still clutched the power that roiled through her veins, but his words gave her pause. When his icy hand landed upon her shoulder, she turned her head ever so slightly and asked, "Why?"

He said, "You might get hurt, but you'll definitely hurt them."

"Isn't that what we want?"

"No," he breathed, the word catching in his throat.

The wraiths hissed in front of her, their forms twisting and writhing in the water. Ros looked between them and the bandit. "What are you not telling us?"

He ignored her, his eyes locked on one wraith who had separated from the others and raised itself in front of Ros. Darian said, "Not these people."

The wraith opened its mouth—her mouth, Ros realized as the shape of the wraith became more defined—

and a breathy, hissing voice said, "They are mine, Darian."

He shook his head. "They have to live."

"I need them, brother. They smell like salt and sunshine and life. I want to feel like that again."

"I know, Cadence. I know. But these people need to keep their lives so they can help save Talabrih."

"Is it worth saving?" the wraith asked.

Darian shrugged. "I don't know. But I have to try. For you and mom. For everyone else who dreamed of something better."

Cadence's eyes flashed toward the others in the water behind Darian, and she said, "I'm so hungry."

"I'm sorry, love."

Ros watched as he continued to stare at her in silence, waiting. She didn't know what to make of the interaction, and she was too unsure of what to say to interfere.

After a few minutes that felt like hours, the wraith said, "They must hurry. I can only hold off my sisters for a few minutes. Today is their only chance to pass these waters. They will not be spared a second time."

"I understand."

"Do you?" Cadence asked. "It grows harder each time, Darian. I cannot promise that a day won't come when I forget who you are to me, who you were, and I drag you into the dark waters to feast on your life, as my sisters did to me."

Rosalinde's gaze shot to Darian as his throat bobbed at the words. He didn't respond, aside from a quick nod of his head. Turning to Ros, he said, "Let's go while we can."

Ros needed no convincing. She pushed forward through the water the last few feet. The rock formations resumed, and with Darian's help, Ros scrambled on top of them. She knelt and reached back to Tancred to help him up, then they joined together to pull Cordelia to safety.

As Ros reached toward Cassian, she caught the frenzied words bantered between him and Darian. "What in the hells was that?"

"We don't have time for this," Darian said.

"If you think I'll let this go—"

"I'll explain it all, but not while we're still in the Deuil. Let's get clear of their domain first." When Cassian's expression darkened, Darian looked into the waters behind them and added, "I swear it on my sister's life—and her cursed afterlife—I will tell you the full truth."

Cassian nodded and climbed onto the stones. His gaze drifted to Rosalinde's outstretched hand, but he didn't take it. The look he gave her was enough for her to pull back from him. When he saw her flinch back, he schooled his face into something softer. But the moment had passed, and each turned from the other.

Ros extended her hand to Darian instead. He took it with a smile and let her help him up. She turned toward the shore, thankful to see Cordelia and her father nearly off the river. With a glance at Darian, she said, "Let's go."

He nodded, but his gaze still searched the dark waters at their feet.

Ros grabbed at his elbow and gave him a shake. "Dar-ian. What are you doing?"

"I'm sorry," he said.

She wasn't sure if he had spoken to her, or the water wraith who had let them pass. Whoever it was, the act of saying those words was enough to pull him from whatever had drawn his attention. Darian turned, gave her a nod, and followed the others.

Four

The companions sat at the edge of the forest. Their skin was dripping wet and cold, but none of them were ready to move into whatever would come next. The silence hung heavy between them, as thick and dark as the trees at their back.

After nearly a quarter of an hour, Darian said, "The wraiths won't follow us on land, but there are other dangers ahead."

"Like what?" Cordelia asked.

"No," Cassian said. "We're not talking about what's in there until you tell us what happened. We can't go forward as unprepared as we were this time."

Darian sighed. "I am truly sorry for that. I hoped we would make it through without seeing them."

"But you knew it was a possibility," Cassian said.

"Of course. That's why I warned you."

Cassian's tone took on an edge as he said, "And yet you didn't tell us of your connection to the wraiths."

"Because it's none of your business."

"You swore on your sister's life—"

"And afterlife," Darian cut in. "Which you witnessed."

Ros said, "The wraith is your sister."

Darian nodded. "Cadence was ten years old when we crossed the Deuil with our mother. I had barely turned fourteen. She took us in the middle of the night, when our father passed out drunk. We had nothing but the clothes on our backs, and each other."

Ros swallowed back the lump forming in her throat. She knew the ending of his story without hearing him speak it; in fact, she would give almost anything if she didn't have to listen to what came next.

"The water had swelled from the rain, but my mother didn't know. She couldn't think beyond getting as far away as possible. So, we pushed forward. We climbed into the water. I made it to the rocks on the far side and climbed up. When I turned to help them, I saw my mother trying to wrestle Cadence away from *something*. I rushed to get back in the water and help her, but they were both pulled under before I could. I ran to the bank and tried to follow as the wraith pulled them downstream, but it was dark, and I lost them."

"Darian," Ros said, reaching a hand out and putting it on his forearm. He jolted at her touch, as if he'd forgotten she was there, lost in his memory.

"I lost them," he repeated.

"It wasn't your fault," she said.

"I could've helped them, saved them, if I'd been paying more attention."

"You were a child," Tancred said.

Darian's gaze turned to him, darkening at the reminder of the king's presence. "They were only two of so, so many. Do you have any idea how many more die like that, fleeing from the dark corners of Talabrih, the parts no one wants to look at? And maybe I couldn't have saved them, but you could have. You *chose* not to."

"It's not that simple," Tancred said.

"It is," Ros replied. All eyes turned to her, surprised. She said, "We don't give our best to those without magic. We treat them as if they aren't as important, and we let the house lords make their own rules, which offer little protection for the groups that are already under-protected."

"We have improved things," Tancred said. "We've tried, at least."

Ros said, "We like to say that we aren't as bad as the Elementalists of the past—and honestly, I'm not certain that's completely true—but that doesn't mean we're better. We are the problem. And until we let the magicless have a seat at the table, we won't find an actual solution."

Despite the story he'd told, the dark memories resting on his brow, Darian's lips curled up ever so slightly. "I never thought I'd hear those words from a noble, much less the future ruler of Talabrih."

"Current ruler," Cassian said.

Tancred's head whipped to him and he asked, "What are you talking about?"

Ros swallowed. She hadn't meant to have this conversation until they were out of danger, until they had secured the throne. "While you were gone—"

"You *took* the throne?"

"I didn't take it. Not intentionally, at least," Ros said, the word flying from her lips. "They appointed me because we didn't have any leads, and the house lords were grumbling amongst themselves. It was all we could do to keep them from revolt."

"Bastards," Tancred mumbled.

"We can return the crown to your head as soon as we get back," she said.

"No," Darian and Cassian said in unison. Darian smiled at that, while Cassian's lips turned down into a deep frown.

Darian said, "The Night house mage doesn't enjoy agreeing with me, but we both recognize the importance of having you remain on the throne. For the magicless, at least."

"The people need you, Ros," Cassian said.

Tancred's brow furrowed at their words. Finally, he asked, "Was I really such a terrible king?"

"Not to my eyes," Cassian said. "You made strides toward equality, but the steps you took were always shy of what they *could* have been. They laid the groundwork for a better future, but Rosalinde is the one who will lead us into that future."

"None of this matters if we can't get to Fire house and find allies," Cordelia said.

"She's right," Darian said, rising to his feet.

"Before we go traipsing through these woods, what else are you hiding?" Cassian asked.

Darian's eyes narrowed, but he said, "Wolves. You know, I've trained them to eat Night mages, so you might have trouble with those."

"Funny," Cas said.

"What do you want from me?" Darian asked. "I'm not sorry for keeping my sister a secret. I barely know you, and what little I do know, I don't like. If I could have avoided telling you about the most traumatic event of my life, I certainly would have. But I was forced to give up that part of myself to strangers. So you'll have to forgive me if I want to keep other things to myself."

"If those things endanger us and our mission, we have the right to know."

Darian sighed. "There could be any number of things in these woods: animals, bandits, Fire house guards and the people fleeing them, errant kings and princesses trying to save kingdoms... There's really no telling what you'll run into on any given day."

Before Cassian could speak up again, Rosalinde said, "We understand, and we trust you to get us past any of those dangers. Please, lead the way so we can reach Fire house while we still have the cover of night on our side."

Darian gave her a nod and set off through the trees. Ros and the others rushed to catch up, the bandit marking a quick pace. The branches intertwined above them, forming a dense canopy. The surrounding darkness was almost complete, silent aside from the rustling of leaves and the distant howl of a wolf.

"Told you," Darian said. "My pets are hungry for Night mage."

Ros suppressed her smile, though Darian's words were spoken so softly that she thought the others probably hadn't heard. She moved closer to Darian as they walked, letting the words tripping through her mind fall out: "I'm sorry about your family. What happened to them was awful."

His step faltered for a moment, unnoticeable if Ros hadn't been beside him. "Thank you," he said. "It was a long time ago."

"Time doesn't dull a loss like that."

"No, it doesn't. I will never stop hurting. But it doesn't drive every decision like it used to."

"Are you sure?"

Darian swallowed. "Not really. I can keep telling myself though, and eventually it'll be true."

"I'm not sure who is left in my family," Ros said. It was the first time she admitted it to herself or anyone else. "I have my father back, but my sister and mother could be lost to me. I won't know until I return to Water house."

Silence settled between them for a moment before Darian said, "You're not what I expected."

"What do you mean?"

"I've heard a lot of stories about the royal family

through the years. Some are more believable than others. The thing that rang true in all of them was selfishness, or at least a lack of acknowledgement for how others are affected by the political decisions."

"That is a fair assessment," Ros said. "I don't think it's intentional, simply an ignorance about what is going on around the kingdom. Sometimes the nobles will petition the crown for something, and we decide based on the information available. Unfortunately, the details rarely encompass everyone affected."

Darian nodded. "That makes sense, and it's nice to hear you acknowledge how that can be a detriment for those involved. That's part of what makes you different; when you speak, you aren't making excuses or trying to justify why things are the way they are. You admit it isn't equal, and even that the crown has made mistakes. It's a refreshing change."

"My father—"

Darian struck his hand through the air and said, "We will never agree where he is concerned."

"It was never malicious," she said.

"He wasted his time on the throne," Darian said. "If you follow that same path, you will, too."

"My path has already diverged from that life."

"Seems that way. You are having a rather civilized and stimulating conversation with a dashing rogue and a wanton scoundrel, after all."

Ros laughed. "An absolute pleasure, by the way."

"Of course it is," he said, an easy smile playing on his

lips. "It's clear you have an easier time with your people than the royals before you. I would wager you've had more interactions with commonfolk in your short years than both of your parents combined."

Memories of sneaking out and running through the streets, hiding in alleys, and spending time with Alaric flooded her mind. "There is no kingdom without the people. Talabrih is nothing but an idea—the people are what shape it into something greater."

"And that is why you'll be a queen for all of us. The Rising Tide has that right about you."

"The Tide?" she asked in a rushed whisper.

He nodded. "You know them, don't you?"

Ros swallowed and said, "I've known some of them, yes."

"They're good people, Ros. All they want is peace, but they're willing to fight to get it if that's what it takes."

"They helped me when I needed them. I wasn't sure what became of them."

Darian gave a casual glance around them before saying, "They're around, or so the rumors say. Rebuilding in the north after the battle at Earth house."

If Darian knew what happened at Earth house, knew about the Rising Tide, then there was far more to him than she suspected. Perhaps he was planted in her path by the Tide for this specific reason. Now she had to figure out how to ask him about it.

They walked for a moment in silence, and as Ros opened her mouth to speak, Darian stopped suddenly, his hand on the hilt of his sword. He held his hand out to quiet her and the others. His voice was barely audible as he asked, "Something's wrong. We're being followed."

Cas asked, "How do you know?"

"I know these woods," he said.

That nonanswer was enough to quiet the Night mage.

Ros's heart raced as she looked around, trying to see through the darkness. "What do we do?"

"We set a trap," Darian replied. His gaze darted between her and Cassian. "Who wants to be bait?"

"I will," Cassian said. His suspicious tone was gone, his words fast and decisive.

Darian motioned for the others to hide behind a nearby thicket, while he and Cassian stayed in the small area cleared of trees—the first they had seen since entering the woods. Darian said, "Stay silent. We don't know what we're up against. Don't come out unless I give you the signal."

"What's the signal?" Ros asked.

"Oh, you'll know it when you hear it."

They waited in silence, the tension in the air almost palpable. Ros could hear her own breathing, slow and steady, as she focused on the sounds of the forest. Time dragged on as they sat in anticipation of their pursuers showing themselves.

Finally, they heard footsteps approaching. Darian's head tilted slightly, but before the figures came into view, Ros heard him whisper, "Fight me."

Ros expected Cassian to question that, since the words

rang through her with surprise. Instead, Cassian swung his fist toward the bandit's face. Darian must have expected more of a delay as well, because he barely pulled himself from Cassian's reach as the night mage's fist flew at him.

"You'll have to do better than that, lordling!" Darian said as six people emerged from the shadows.

Initially Ros thought they were more bandits, possibly even from the same group they had encountered earlier, but her eyes caught on the polished boots they all wore, on the perfect posture they held, and the way they positioned themselves in a formation to guard one another. *Guards,* she thought, *or mercenaries.* Neither were good for their mission to make it to Fire house.

"What's going on here?" the woman in the front asked. She was bronze-skinned, with short brown hair and a heart-shaped face. Her frame was short, her body petite, but Ros noted the muscles corded along her arms, the way her shoulders looked as solid as granite.

"Having some fun with the little rich boy," Darian said, a lazy smile tilting his mouth.

The woman put her hand on her sword—a finely crafted thing, if the hilt was any indication—and said, "Fun is over. He's coming with us."

Darian's expression shifted seamlessly from his casual smile to one of outrage. "Now wait one minute," he said. "This is *my* quarry, and I'll get what I want. Find your own lost lord to rob."

The woman motioned with two fingers, and a brutish man behind her stepped forward. Darian and Cas both tensed as the man walked toward them, but his hand landed on the money pouch at his waist rather than the row of knives strapped down his barrel chest. The man pulled out three coins and tossed them on the ground in front of Darian. Though Ros did not see what denomination the coins were, she noticed the way Darian's eyes went wide in surprise.

"Disarm him and be on your way."

"Well," he said, picking up the coins at his feet and pocketing them the next second. Darian cast a quick look at Cassian, then released the sword belted to his waist, saying, "I guess he's yours now."

The woman smirked. "Don't spend it all in one place."

Darian backed away from the group, hands in the air. "Don't worry about that. My money, my poor decisions. In fact, I think I'll head straight to the nearest tavern to drink away my troubles."

Then he was gone, disappeared into the forest as if he'd never been there.

A tall redheaded man laughed as he shook his head. "He was something, wasn't he?"

"Aye, Callum, exactly your type—a scoundrel, and a waste of our time," another man said.

Callum smiled. "That is exactly the sort of man I like. Especially when he's as pretty as that one. Right, Torin? Or do you prefer this one?" he asked, motioning to Cassian.

The brutish man's cheeks reddened, but he said nothing. The woman in front pursed her lips, cutting off their banter. "Stop with your nonsense."

"Just having a laugh to ease the tension now that the chase is over," Callum said.

"That was too easy."

"Be thankful, Ash," the big man said. "We usually have to work a lot harder for our prize."

"And for a lot less pay," Callum added.

Ash said, "You celebrate and act like fools, as if our job is done. This mage is only one of those we seek. Get your shit together until we have the others, or I'll end you myself." A silent moment passed between the people behind her, each of them casting glances at the ground or the dark trees around them—anywhere but toward Ash. Though she didn't look satisfied with what had happened, Ash let the moment pass. Her face settled back into something pinched as she said, "Coen, Delise, restrain the mage."

A look of panic crossed Cassian's face as the two who had been silent so far moved to subdue him. Ros watched him scan the surrounding forest for anything that could help. There was nowhere to run, and though he was a gifted swordsman, he certainly couldn't fight all six of his attackers. Especially not without his magic, which was unusable since they had crossed the river and entered into the Fire house wards. She was preparing to jump out from the thicket when she heard a rich baritone call out from the darkness, "On second thought, I don't have nearly enough troubles to drink away. I should definitely make some more. Right, Princess?"

As Ros, Tancred, and Cordelia jumped out from their

hiding place, Darian appeared behind Ash's group, sword drawn and arcing overhead before anyone had time to react. He moved with fluid grace, his sword flashing in a sliver of moonlight coming through the canopy as he sliced through two of them—Coen and Delise, it seemed—in quick succession.

Ros focused on another of the bandits, pulling two knives from her bandolier and throwing them at the man's legs. The knives hit their mark, causing the bandit to stumble and fall, blood gushing from his calf. He crawled out of view, and though she knew she should search for him, there was too much going on to worry about him right now.

With a roar that surprised his daughter, Tancred joined the fray. He charged forward with his short sword raised high, bringing it down with a powerful swing that Callum barely managed to parry. She watched the two for a few seconds, readying her knives to intervene. When Tancred spun Callum's back toward her, Ros struck. Her knife jutted from his liver. As he doubled over in pain, Tancred used the distraction to knock him out.

Brutish Torin, recovering from the initial shock, unsheathed his own sword and moved toward Darian, determined to protect his company. The growl that came from him was enough to send a jolt of fear through Ros, but Darian somehow managed a rakish smile as the man approached.

"I'm going to hurt you," Torin said.

"Give it a try, big boy. Maybe I'll like it."

Torin stopped in his tracks, eyes widening as his cheeks burned red once again. Ros didn't watch them further, knowing that whatever Darian had planned for the poor man would be far worse than anything she could do.

Her gaze found Ash, who dove sword first toward Cassian. The Night house mage lunged for the sword that Darian had loosed from his side. Once retrieved, he was a blur of motion, his blade striking with precision and speed. He fought with a controlled fury, his movements efficient and deadly. Ash was equally skilled with her blade, and they moved between attacking and defending, with neither seeming to have the upper hand.

A few minutes later, Darian sidled up to Rosalinde's side. He was sweating and dirty, but a grin split his face. She asked, "What happened to Torin?"

"Who?"

"The big guy."

"Oh, he's fine. He let me tie him up."

"Let you?" Ros asked, eyebrows raising.

"I mean, he struggled a bit, but we both knew it was for show."

A laugh bubbled up from Ros, and she quickly covered her mouth, feeling like it wasn't the right time for such things.

"It's fine to laugh, Princess," Darian said, brows furrowing at her reaction. "Natural, really, because I'm hilarious."

"Probably not the time," she said.

He shrugged. Pointing to Ash and Cassian, he said, "Any idea when they'll be finished?"

"They're evenly matched."

"Quite," Tancred said, stepping to Rosalinde's other side.

"We could help," Darian said. "But I get the impression your man would not be happy with that."

As if in answer, Cassian cast a withering look toward Darian. It cost him. Ash got inside his guard. Before she could press her advantage, Rosalinde's hand shot to the blades belted to her chest. She threw them with quick precision, thanks to years of practice learning to aim her magic. The knives buried into the woman's leg, one of them slicing the tendon behind her knee. She fell to the ground, her sword clattering away.

Darian moved to stand over the fallen leader, his sword pointed at the Ash's throat. "You picked the wrong group to follow," he said. "Now, tell me why you're here."

Ash coughed, blood trickling from a wound on her lip. "We were sent to capture you," she said, her voice laced with venom. "There's a bounty on your heads. Someone doesn't want you reaching Fire house."

"Who?" Ros demanded, stepping forward.

Ash shook her head. "I don't know. We were given orders to stop you. A letter. Anonymous, paid in advance."

Darian's eyes narrowed. "You're of no use to us."

He raised his sword, and the woman flinched, but Ros said, "No. Killing her is pointless."

"She can report back on our whereabouts," Darian said.

"To whom? She doesn't know who hired them."

"I don't like it. There will be more of them, and we can't afford to be delayed. If they find her and she tells them what she knows..."

"We give mercy when we can," Ros said. "We show them—"

"Help." The voice was weak, barely there. Ros and the others turned toward the sound to see Cordelia dragging herself toward them. A bloody knife protruded from her side—one of the very knives Ros had strapped to her chest.

Five

Tancred jumped to her side faster than anyone else could react, but his healing magic was useless inside the Fire house wards. He put pressure on the wound, but blood quickly coated the king's fingers, and Cordelia's face was pale.

"Cordelia!" Ros cried, rushing to her.

Cassian and Darian remained where they were, swords pointed at the attackers who were conscious. Tone urgent and tight with worry, Cassian said, "We need to get her to Fire house, now!"

King Tancred nodded, taking command as he would in his clinic. "Cassian, carry her. Darian, lead the way. We can't afford to waste any time."

"What about them?" Darian asked, pointing toward Ash.

Ros knew what he wanted. She could see it on his face, in the clench of his jaw, but she would not authorize their deaths when they were not warranted. These people were looking for work, hoping for a way to eat and help those they loved; it just so happened that Ros and her group had been the target this time. Perhaps their way of life wasn't one Ros would choose, but it was difficult to know for sure since she had never faced the things they had.

"Let them go," she said.

Darian groaned. "That's a bad idea, Princess."

"We're not killing them."

"They would kill us if they had the chance," Darian said. "Your friend is proof of that."

His words rang true. The wound in Cordelia's side had surely come from the man Ros had let crawl into the forest with her knives stuck in his leg. She sighed and said, "Lucky for them we're living by different rules."

"Different rules between our kind and yours are the reason we have to resort to these jobs," Ash said, her voice tinged with hatred.

Ros nodded. She agreed with the woman, and would love nothing more than to sit down with her and try to hash out a way to fix things for *all* of Talabrih. But she didn't have time. Cordelia was losing too much blood, and they needed to move.

"We'll leave you untied so that you can gather the rest of your group before the wild things in this wood come for you. Heed my warning: if you persist in tracking and hindering us, we cannot continue to show you mercy."

"Mercy?" Ash asked, a bitter laugh barking from her.

"You think that sending us back empty-handed to whatever monster has paid for our services will be a mercy?"

"It's more than you deserve," Darian said.

"We must go," Tancred said. He and Cassian were already leaving their small clearing, Cordelia in tow.

"I hope we meet again under better circumstances," Ros said. "I believe I could learn a lot from you."

Ash gave nothing but a growl as Ros and Darian ran after the others. They caught up quickly, and Darian moved past them to show them the fastest route to Fire house. Ros wasn't sure what the consequences of showing up at their gates with an injured daughter of the flame would be, but they were out of options.

Heart pounding in her chest, Ros glanced back to make sure Ash and her band weren't following. They moved swiftly through the forest; the underbrush tore at Rosalinde's clothes as they pushed forward. The urgency of their mission fueled their speed, and every second ticked away like a drumbeat in Rosalinde's ears.

After what felt like an eternity, the trees thinned, and the imposing gates of Fire house came into view. Ros's heart leaped with relief. "There it is," she shouted. "Only a little further!"

Cordelia's breathing was shallow, and her eyes fluttered open and closed as she struggled to stay conscious. "Stay with us, Cordelia," Cassian murmured, his voice full of desperation. "We're almost there."

Ros felt a lump form in her throat. They couldn't lose Cordelia—not after everything they'd been through. She pushed herself harder, her legs burning with the effort. They burst from the forest and onto the open grounds approaching Fire house. The tall spires loomed overhead, casting long shadows as the sun set.

Cassian started forward, but Darian threw a hand against his chest. Only a few feet ahead, a sheer drop-off greeted them, with a wide moat of churning lava and fire surrounding the castle. It hadn't been visible from the forest's edge, but as they eased forward, the intense heat radiated upwards, causing Ros to take a step back instinctively. She knew the moat was here, had seen it from the road when they'd visited in the past, but this vantage point offered a completely new view of it. One she didn't like, and one they couldn't cross without access to their magic.

Cassian gritted his teeth and asked, "What now?" He panted, glancing around for a solution.

"There's a bridge by the main gate," Tancred said, pointing to the right where a stone structure arched over the fiery moat. "But it's guarded."

Ros's heart stuttered in her chest. They didn't have time for a confrontation. Cordelia's life depended on their speed. "We have to risk it," she said, determination hardening her voice.

As they made their way toward the crossover, the heat grew more oppressive. Ros could feel the sweat trickling down her back, but she forced herself to focus. This was their only way across.

They reached the bridge, and Ros could see the guards more clearly now—tall, armored figures with weapons at the ready. One of them spotted the group and raised an alarm, drawing the attention of the others.

"Stay close," King Tancred commanded, placing his hand on his pommel. "And be ready to fight."

With hearts pounding and adrenaline surging, they stepped onto the stone walkway. "We need help!" Ros shouted, waving her arms frantically. She hoped their call for help would disarm the guards, but with her father drawing his sword, she wasn't sure anything would calm them.

"Stop where you are," a guard called.

Ros and her group stopped halfway across the bridge. She yelled, "Send a Healer!" When no one moved to do anything, she added, "We have Lady Cordelia in tow, and she's been injured."

One guard pushed through the others and crossed the span between them in an instant. As he ran, he yanked off his helmet and tossed it to the side, revealing Cordelia's cousin, Dryden. It had only been a few weeks since Ros had seen the mage at the Great Match, but everything about him had changed in that short time. His blond curls had been shorn away, leaving only stubble. His cleanly shaved face now sported a scraggly beard, mostly blond, but with splotches of red and brown as well. More than his physical attributes, though, Dryden had a *look* about him; he was exhausted.

"What happened?" he asked.

"Bandits," Ros said.

Dryden cast her a quick glance, followed by a second,

longer look when he realized who stood before him. "Queen Rosalinde, forgive me—"

"No need," she said, cutting off the formalities before he could fall into old habits. "Get help for Cordelia. We will wait here until there is time for the Lord Ruler to decide what he wishes to do with us."

"The Lord Ruler," Dryden breathed, his words catching in his throat. "You haven't heard."

Rosalinde's brow furrowed, but she said, "News can wait, but Cordelia can't."

Dryden gave her a nod. "Follow me." He turned and marched toward Fire house. One of the guards in his path protested, but without a word in response, a thunderclap echoed around them. Anything they might have said was cut off, and the remaining guards parted to let the group pass.

They crossed under the arch that led from the bridge and outer walls into a massive courtyard. As soon as they were within the walls, a group of people rushed toward them, their faces a mix of concern and curiosity. One of them, a tall black woman with long white braids, stepped forward. "What's happened?" she demanded, her eyes sharp as she took in the scene.

"Sloane," Dryden breathed, clearly glad to see her. "They need a Healer."

"She's hurt," Cassian said, his voice strained as he gently shifted so they could see Cordelia's face.

Murmurs instantly rose upon seeing Cordelia. The white-haired woman ignored them, snapping into action.

"Bring her inside. We'll take care of her." She turned to Dryden as she was leading them away and said, "Find the Lord Ruler."

They followed her into Fire house, the cool air a stark contrast to the heat outside. The woman led them down a series of corridors to a large room filled with medical supplies. Healers bustled about, tending to various patients.

"Over here," the woman called, directing them to a cot in the corner.

Cassian carefully placed Cordelia on the cot, and the Healers immediately began their work. Ros watched anxiously, her hands clenched at her sides. King Tancred stood beside her, his face drawn with worry.

"We did the right thing coming here," he whispered, as much to himself as to Ros. "Maybe not the way we wanted to arrive."

"It doesn't matter what we wanted, this is what we've got," Ros said.

Tancred nodded. "They'll be able to help her."

Ros swallowed, unable to shake the knot of fear in her stomach. She glanced at Cassian, who was watching the Healers intently.

"She's strong," Ros said, her voice firm. "She'll pull through this."

They stood together, united in their worry for Cordelia. The Healers worked swiftly, their hands moving with practiced precision. Time seemed to stretch as they waited, each moment feeling like an eternity. After several minutes, Ros heard footsteps running toward them. She turned to see Dryden enter the room, and at his side was... Florian?

"Where is she?" Florian boomed, his eyes flashing.

Sloane stepped between him and Rosalinde's group, hands raised. "Calm down, Lord Ruler. The Healers have her."

"Calm down?" he growled. "My sister is brought in barely clinging to life after missing for months, and you want me to *calm down*?"

"It won't help her to see you this way. She needs her brother, not her lord."

Florian's jaw clenched at her words, but he gave a terse nod. He swallowed, as if forcing his rage and fear back down his throat. "Is she... will she be..."

One of the Healers stepped to Sloane's side, her expression serious but not without hope. "She's stable for now, but she needs rest and continued care. She got here just in time."

"Thank the elements," Ros said.

Her words drew Florian's attention, and he turned his golden gaze to her. He blinked several times, trying to reconcile what his eyes were showing him. Finally, tripping over his words a bit, he asked, "My queen?"

Ros gave him a tentative smile. "Lord le Fevre. I'm glad to see you."

Florian's brows knit together as he said, "You shouldn't be. I have orders to arrest you on sight."

"Good thing you're not much for following orders," she said.

Florian blinked again, unsure. "You... you brought my sister home?"

Ros nodded. "We rescued her from Air house. We've been making our way here since, but we were attacked in the woods."

Florian raised his hands to silence her words, glancing around. "Let's take this conversation elsewhere."

"Like the dungeons?" Cassian asked, his mouth tilting up in a smirk.

"Is that where you Night mages feel most comfortable?"

Ros looked between the two men who glared at one another for another moment before both of their faces broke out in grins. Cas said, "It's good to see you."

"And you, though you've arrived at the absolute worst time."

"Why is that?" Cassian asked. "Maybe we can help."

Florian shook his head. "I don't know if there's anything any of us can do."

Ros asked, "What's wrong?"

Florian looked between Ros and Cassian, saying, "We're broken, in shambles." His voice cracked as he said, "Fire house is burning."

Six

After giving strict instructions to Sloane and the Healers regarding his sister, Florian led Ros, Cassian, Tancred, and Darian through the inner corridors of Fire house. Ros had been to the fiery city before, but it had been many years, and she had only seen the "pretty" parts. It was always that way for a royal; Ros was never allowed to see what was real, only what was deemed suitable for someone of her station. It was the same way at Water house, and all the other houses, she presumed. These secret corridors running through Fire house were off limits to a visiting royal, but the fastest way to travel with an ally who could help your burning city.

They climbed three flights of steps and exited onto the rampart. Flickering light from blazing parts of Fire house cast eerie shadows on their faces, revealing a mixture of fear, rage, and determination. The air was thick with smoke and the scent of charred wood; the distant sounds of clashing metal and shouted orders told them that the battle was far from over.

How did I miss this on the way in? she thought. The answer was simple; Ros and the others had been so preoccupied with saving Cordelia that they'd missed the signs of battle around them. Dryden in a guard's armor should have tipped her off that something was wrong, but nothing had mattered in those crucial moments.

Florian's face was a mask of grim resolve as he turned to face them. Voice strained, he stated the obvious: "Fire house is under attack."

Ros felt a chill run down her spine. "Who is attacking?"

Florian shook his head. "We don't know. They came out of nowhere, overwhelming our defenses. We've pushed them back, but we're losing ground."

"Magic?" Darian asked.

Florian sighed. "Hard to say. I've had a few reports that there were magic wielders, but nothing confirmed. There's a lot of confusion about what people are seeing. Some claim there are mages from every house, that those currently holding the throne have sent them to destroy us..." He trailed off, shaking his head. "I don't know what to believe. Then when you showed up—"

"Suspicious timing," Ros said.

Florian winced. "Not that I think you would do something like this."

Ros put her hand on Florian's arm and said, "I wouldn't blame you if you did. There's a lot going on."

He put his hand on hers and said, "You are my queen, but more than that, you are my friend. I trust you."

Cassian's eyes flicked down momentarily, but rose back to meet Florian's gaze as he said, "We're here to help."

"I know. And I'm grateful."

Tancred cleared his throat and said, "I despise myself for asking, but I must: what has become of your father?"

"I don't know," Florian said, his lips pressing into a thin line. "He was with the warriors, who went out to meet the first wave of attackers. Again, conflicting reports have returned to me. Some say he went down in battle, others that he was captured. One person swore he was still fighting and would not take a break until every attacker met his flame. We haven't seen his body, alive or dead, so I have no way of knowing what to believe."

"Why would he go out?" Darian asked. "It would make more sense for him to command from behind the scenes."

"He refused to send our warriors against an enemy he would not face himself."

"Brave fool," Darian muttered.

"Sloane called you by his title," Tancred said.

Florian nodded. "He signed over his title and responsibilities as soon as the first attack started. I wanted to fight, but I wasn't permitted. Father said he was needed on the field, I was needed to protect our home, and he wouldn't listen to reason."

"Most of the castle is still intact," Darian said. It was a statement, not a question, and Ros wondered how he had assessed such a thing with as little as they had seen. Still, Florian nodded his agreement to Darian's words.

"Is the sanctum secure?" Cassian asked, his grip tightening on his sword hilt.

Florian glanced between them. "We've deflected every attempt to overtake it, but just barely. We need to find a better way to secure it permanently. If the attackers break through to the very heart of Fire house, to the sacred place where we guard all that is most dear to our people, we'll lose everything."

"What do you have in there that is so special?" Darian asked.

Florian swallowed. "I mean no offense in saying this, but I cannot reveal those secrets to those who are not part of my house."

Darian stepped forward. "That's fine. We'll figure it out after we save your ass."

"What about the wounded?" Tancred asked, drawing Florian's attention. "Are they safe?"

Florian swallowed, and Ros knew his thoughts had briefly turned to his sister. "They're as safe as they can get. Sloane moved most of the Healers and their patients to an inner corridor. The place you saw was their outside unit to be closer for those needing immediate triage. Once the injured are stable, they get moved to a secure location."

"I would like to go to them," Tancred said. "That's where I'll be the most helpful."

Florian nodded. "I'll take you there myself."

Ros said, "The rest of us will go to the sanctum to see what we can do."

"Thank you," Florian said. He pointed into the distance, too close to some of the highest flames. "The entrance is through there."

Cassian cursed. "They're closing in."

"You're with a daughter of Water house," Ros said. "Let the fire burn. It will not touch us."

"Can you reach your magic inside the wards?" Darian asked.

Ros tugged at the magic in her veins. "I feel it, though it seems far away."

"Right," Florian said. "I can fix that. Give me your hand."

Ros placed her hand in his, and Florian let the tip of his index finger rest in the center of her palm. After a few seconds of nothing happening, a prick of pain burned her skin. It built a moment longer until Ros was ready to pull from Florian's grip. Finally, when she thought she couldn't take anymore, he released her.

"Apologies. I had to burn through the enchantment." He reached for Cassian, who presented his hand. Florian did the same thing to Cassian, but after only a few seconds, his head tilted to the side and his face contorted in confusion. He released Cassian's hand and said, "The wards were barely more than a thought covering your magic. Honestly, if you hadn't known to expect them to reject your power, I think you could have used your abilities inside the shield."

"Why?" Cassian asked, his confusion mirroring Florian's.

"I'm not sure. Something to wonder about once we're out of this mess. Until then, be careful—the enemy is everywhere." Florian gave a quick nod to Ros, Cassian, and Darian. "King Tancred, follow me."

As Florian disappeared into the chaos with Tancred, the others exchanged nervous glances. Darian said, "This won't be easy."

"It never is," Ros said, sighing.

With a shrug, Cassian said, "I don't know. I had a pretty relaxed way of life until I came to the Great Match."

"All downhill after that, huh?" she asked.

"Oh, I wouldn't say that. There have definitely been some perks."

Darian cleared his throat. "If you two could stop flirting while we're in mortal danger, I'd really like to get going."

Ros felt her cheeks heat as Cassian gave her a sly smile and said, "I don't know what you're talking about. I was simply pointing out that Queen Rosalinde has a history of getting herself into dangerous situations."

Darian rolled his eyes. "Right."

"Let's go," Ros said. She turned from both men and headed into the heart of Fire house.

THE CENTRAL HALL was a scene of utter devastation. Flames licked at the walls, and the once-grand banners of Fire house lay in tatters on the ground. Mages and guards fought desperately against shadowy figures that seemed to melt in and out of the darkness.

"Night house?" Ros asked, gaze shooting to Cassian, who wore a look of utter horror at the shadows.

He gave a terse shake of his head. "No. Their magic... I would feel it if they were from Night house."

"You're certain?"

Cassian nodded. "I've always been able to feel the shadows, to control them. They speak to me, even when I'd rather they didn't." He paused, brows knitting together. "There has only been one exception."

"Gaius," she whispered.

Cassian didn't respond, but Ros didn't need him to. Without a word of either acknowledgment or denial, it was clear that Cassian's thoughts were on his brother.

"Don't get lost in those thoughts now," she said. "We'll sort it out. For now, let's just focus on getting into the sanctum."

Ros opened her palm toward the fire, summoning a gust of wind that extinguished some of the flames blocking their way. She moved forward, scanning their path for threats. "Stay close."

They only made it ten paces before they were surrounded. Shadows rose on all sides, blocking out the faintest hint of light but never touching them.

"What in the hells is this?" Darian asked.

Cassian's brows knit together in confusion. His right hand reached toward the shadows, fingers splayed apart as he sent his power into the void. Seconds later, a shudder passed through him. His voice was strained as he said, "I've never known darkness like this." Ros lifted her fingers, as if to reach for the shadows with her own magic, but Cassian seized her hand and pushed it down. "Don't. There's something wrong within this barren murk, and I wouldn't have it clinging to you."

"Will it attach itself to you?" she asked.

He tilted his head, shaking it slightly. "I have lived with shadows for all of my life; though these are not the same, I can find my way free of any that try to entwine themselves with me. If anything, they should fear that I will cling to them."

"Can we go through them?" Darian asked.

"No," Cassian said. "It's too risky."

Darian asked, "Can you dispel it?"

Cassian shook his head. "My magic calls to the shadows, not the other way around. I can banish my own, but not this gloom."

"Maybe I can," Ros said.

Darian's brows knit together as he asked, "How would a Water house mage accomplish such a feat?"

Ros moved her wrist so that the ruby bracelet Ombretta had given her came into view. Surrounded by shadows, it didn't shine and sparkle. It didn't need to. Ros knew she could call on the power stored there and be answered with the gifts of Fire.

"Where did you get that?" Cassian asked. "I've seen you wearing it since you came back from Faerie."

"Your mother," Ros said. She tried to smile, to acknowledge to him how kind Ombretta had been with this gift, but it didn't reach her eyes. "She gave it to me before she went back to Faerie, to use when I needed help from her house."

"We've established that Night house gifts won't work," Cassian said.

Ros winced as she said, "Your mother isn't native to Night house."

"What are you talking about?" he asked.

"In Faerie, your uncle Lucasian is the Prince of Shadows. Ombretta wields Fire magic."

"That makes little sense," Cas said. "To breed my particular kind of magic—"

Darian interrupted, saying, "As fascinating as this is, can we sort out your parental trauma later? We're in a bit of a hurry to make it to the sanctum. So, if you have a way to get us there, it doesn't really matter where it came from, just how you use it."

Ros nodded. She closed her eyes and held up her hand toward the shadows, letting her thoughts turn to fire, flame, and light. She felt the bracelet warm against her skin. Ros let the heat build until it was nearly unbearable. It was then that she felt a hand on her shoulder, and she opened her eyes. Hand still raised, Ros watched as light streamed from her palm, creating a path through the shadows that fled from the bracelet's power.

"Let's go," she said, her teeth gritted against the blistering pain of the hot metal pressing on her skin.

Cassian took Rosalinde's free hand in his and pulled her through the hallway of light she created. The shadows gathered behind them as they passed, but dared not cross into the radiance she generated.

Halfway across the courtyard, the shadows disappeared. They hadn't passed through them or out of their range—they were simply gone. Ros let the light fall, relieving the pain on her wrist. She had one brief second of reprieve before realizing that the wall of shadows had been replaced by something far, far worse. All around them were mages dressed in colors from every house, representing Water, Earth, Air, Fire, and Night.

Ros looked into the eyes of those around her, searching for any reason they were there, joined together to attack Fire house. Every stare met her with the same answer: they weren't there. Ros, Cassian, and Darian were facing an army of the dead.

Seven

"What is this madness?" Darian whispered.

"I've read stories," Cassian said, "but I didn't believe there was any truth to them."

"I was hoping it was just my imagination," Ros said.

"No such luck," Darian said.

Cassian swallowed hard and said, "We're surrounded by Hollows."

"What defeats a Hollow in those old stories?" Darian asked.

"Nothing," Cassian said.

Ros cast a glance toward the sanctum. They were so close, but not close enough when encircled by an army of undead. She said, "There was always one common denominator in those stories: someone is controlling them."

Cas locked eyes with her, understanding dawning on his face. "Gaius."

Darian looked between them. "Who?"

"My brother."

"You have a necromancer brother and never thought to ask how to defeat his armies of undead, just in case?"

"He's not a necromancer," Cassian said.

Darian gestured toward the horde and said, "I beg to differ."

Before Cas could retort, Ros cut in, saying, "Why aren't they attacking?"

Both men turned and looked at the throng. As the three of them stared at those surrounding them, none could find an answer for why they were able to stand unmolested amongst them.

"It's a perfect circle," Darian said, pointing at the ground around them.

Ros spun around, confirming his words. It truly was an absolutely flawless circle. She said, "I have an idea."

With the men following her lead, Ros stepped toward the sanctum. As she moved, so did the Hollows; with Ros as a fixed point in the center, the undead kept a circumference around her that never changed, never drew closer or farther away.

"I don't understand," Darian said.

"They aren't allowed to hurt Rosalinde," Cassian said.

"But why?"

"To toy with me," Ros said. "Gaius has delusions of what we could do together, and he thinks he can harass me into joining him."

Darian scrubbed a hand over his face. "Why in all the

65

hells did I try to rob you of all people? I could've stolen from some petty lord and been home already."

"Nothing is coincidence," Cassian said. "As loath as I am to admit it, there's a reason for your presence here."

"Yeah, I'm a damned fool who can't stay out of trouble," Darian muttered.

Ros smiled. "This is one delight of befriending me. I have often been accused of walking hand-in-hand with peril."

"Good to know. Would've been nice information to have a few hours ago, but I guess it makes sense considering what has happened in the short time I've been around you."

"You get used to it," Cassian said, the corners of his lips curling up in a smile.

Ros smacked at his shoulder, a lightness blooming between them that felt strange in view of the things they were facing. The kingdom was in shambles with infighting and bordering on war, the lower class was poised to erupt and needed help, literal monsters were surrounding them and being controlled by an evil mage, and the only thing consistent for any of them was the presence of chaos.

"What do you think will happen if we continue moving toward the sanctum?" Darian asked. "Will they shift around you, or will they eventually stop you?"

"Only one way to find out," Ros said. She advanced a few steps in the direction of the sanctum. The undead army shifted around her but left the circle of space intact. Feeling more confident, Ros took a few more steps, putting her within thirty paces of the sanctum. The dead mages stopped moving. As Ros stood face to face with one of them, she could see thin black lines of shadow tracing down their face. If she'd had any doubt that Gaius was involved, it was gone now.

"I guess you found their limit," Cassian said.

"What now?" Darian asked.

The three glanced back and forth with each other, then Ros took a deep breath and said, "We push through."

Back to back, swords drawn, they moved as one, cutting down the enemies who stood in their path. The undead retaliated with the magic they held while alive: fire burned against Rosalinde's skin, water and air created walls that pushed against them, the ground crackled and puckered beneath their feet in little earthquakes that were pale comparisons of what the mages could have done in life. And then there was Night house. Tendrils of darkness erupted throughout the assembly, reaching for them as they pressed their way across the courtyard. Bodies moved in and out of the shadows, only able to shadow-walk in short distances. Shadows leaped up before them and disappeared at the same moment. The undead weren't there to harm them; they were there to distract them.

"They're weak," Rosalinde said. "They only contain a fraction of the power they had in life."

Darian said, "They're just here to slow us down."

"And it's working. We've barely made any progress," Ros said.

"Why? What are they keeping us from?" Cassian asked.

Ros met his gaze, then turned back to face the sanctum. Whatever reason Gaius had for stalling them, they needed to press forward and figure it out before it was too late. She swallowed hard, knowing that the question she was about to pose to Cassian was a lot—too much—but she had to ask. "You need to take control of them and move them out of our way."

He shook his head, immediately rejecting what she proposed. "I can't."

"You can. You share the same powers as your brother."

Cassian pressed his lips into a thin line, his eyes going dark as he replied, "Fine then, maybe I can. But I won't."

"We need them out of the way. Now," Darian said. "If you can do it, you should."

"I will not defile myself or my house by doing such a thing. My brother shames us enough without me adding to it."

Ros saw the resolution on his face. Cassian would not be convinced, no matter what she said. He wanted to protect his house and the image the rest of Talabrih had of them; turning them into necromancers in the minds of the kingdom, even in a situation this dire, would not do.

So Ros reached for her own power. She had absorbed the Night Cradle, and had access to its power. Though she had given up that part of Lucasian that had taught her how to access it, she still knew where to reach for that power and use the knowledge he had imparted to her. Ros closed her eyes and murmured a silent plea to the Tuath Dé to give her what she needed at this moment. Her heart dared to believe he was in a position to answer her, but more than that, she hoped he was safe.

As Ros reached deep into the well of shadows in her mind, she felt the cold, dark tendrils of power coil around her thoughts. The darkness caressed her senses, coating over them with an oily sheen that felt both like an old friend saying hello and an unmentionable temptation that she knew to avoid. The shadows curled into her consciousness like a silent companion that whispered forgotten secrets and forbidden knowledge. Her mind became a vast, echoing chasm where light could not tread, and within that void, she found what she needed.

Ros imagined the shadows like a living entity, writhing and undulating in the depths of her consciousness. Each thread of darkness pulsed with an ancient rhythm, a beat that matched the steady thrum of her heart. They were not merely a tool; they were an extension of her will, a force that bent to her command.

As she called upon them, the power surged through her, filling her veins with resolve. Rosalinde reached for the strand of magic that held the undead; it was a tentative thing, barely holding onto them, as if the mages it controlled were little more than an afterthought and meant nothing to that awful power. Ros dug shadowy claws into that alien magic and shook, shredding the hold it had over the dead mages until it was no more. Once released from Gaius' power, she could feel the souls surrounding her, restless and forgotten, drawn to her like moths to a flame. They yearned for release, for purpose, and she was their mistress, their harbinger. The weight of their sorrow, their rage, and their despair settled heavily upon her, but she did not falter. They had wished her no harm, had not wanted to do what the necromancer had forced upon them, and now they begged her for freedom from their plight.

The darkness swelled within her, and she reached out with her mind, commanding the shadows that bound those undead mages to her will to seep into the earth, to return the essence taken from the bones and the remnants of the fallen. She felt the ground tremble around her as the dead responded. The shadows wrapped around them disintegrated, removing what bound them to her will and animated them with unnatural vigor.

A sense of satisfaction filled her as the army of undead disassembled before her, their empty eyes sparking with a dark light that flickered in thank you before fading for the last time. Their souls released into the ether. She knew that this power came at a cost, and though she had done what was right and released the dead to a peaceful end, the shadows would exact their price in time.

Ros blinked as the shadows receded from her mind. Cas and Darian stared at the space around them, brows knit in confusion, and as she looked out onto a yard of bones, she wondered how it had looked to them. She felt as if she'd been locked in the shadows for days, but it was clear that barely a minute had passed. Just long enough for the army to fall.

"Let's go. We've wasted enough time," Ros said.

Cassian looked up, his eyes searching hers. "What have you done?"

Ros shook her head. "What you couldn't."

She cast her hand forward, sending a gale of wind that blew the bones from their path. Ros crossed the space to the sanctum's heavy wooden doors. Just before she pressed open the doors, a voice cracked through the air like a whip, power dripping from the word as it commanded, "Stop."

Ros turned to see Gilthroy le Fevre standing on the other side of the courtyard. The fire mage stood tall, his presence commanding and formidable. His tanned skin bore the marks of a life lived playing with flames, weathered and lined with age, yet still strong. Gilthroy's rugged, angular face, carved with years of experience, exuded both wisdom and an unyielding resolve. His fair hair, streaked with silver, was pulled back at the nape of his neck, the loose strands catching the light of the flames that danced around him.

The air surrounding him shimmered with heat, distorting the space as waves of energy radiated outward. The flames responded to his presence, crackling with a life of their own, as if eager to obey his every command. They clung to his form, flickering in and out of existence, casting his features in an ever-changing light. His eyes, intense and focused, glowed with an inner fire, reflecting the power that surged within him.

Around his hands, the flames spiraled and twisted, forming intricate patterns of searing heat. He moved toward them, and each step was accompanied by a burst of flame, the fire swirling around him like a living, breathing entity. The heat was palpable, radiating from his very being, making the air thick and heavy. His power was not just something he wielded; it was a part of him, an extension of his very soul.

Ros had never seen anything like it. She had witnessed elementalists using their gifts, had seen them at their strongest and most powerful, but this display was something altogether different. Gilthroy wasn't using the power of Fire house, he was the very embodiment of the element itself.

As he stood there, surrounded by the raw, untamed energy, he was the incarnation of destruction and creation. The flames did not burn him—they revered him, bowing to his will, a testament to the mastery he had achieved over the years. In his presence, the world seemed to hold its breath, as if recognizing the sheer magnitude of the force he commanded.

"We are here to help," Rosalinde said, stepping forward.

"You will not enter the holy sanctum of my house," he said.

She looked for any flicker of darkness, any sign that Gilthroy was under Gaius' influence, but she saw none.

Ros nodded, summoning all her strength to be ready in case she needed to defend herself and her friends. She felt the familiar surge of power as she called upon the elements, and left that tingling energy burning at her fingertips, ready to be unleashed.

"We do not wish you any harm," she said. "Nor harm to any of your house."

"Easy words from the lips of a liar," Gilthroy spat.

Rosalinde's brows furrowed. "Your son asked for our help."

"My son?" Gilthroy asked, eyes narrowing. "How dare you speak of him after seeing to his murder?"

Ros jolted at the words. "Murder? No, it can't be. We were with him minutes ago and he was fine."

"More lies," Gilthroy said. "My spies reported his death more than an hour ago. Dead at the hands of the Water house princess, they said."

"There's been a mistake," Cassian said, stepping forward.

The flames surrounding Gilthroy dimmed and flickered at the sight of the Night house mage. His face contorted, his voice a strangled whisper as he said, "You... you're here. Cassian... my boy..."

Cassian's head tilted at his words, unsure. He asked, "Lord le Fevre?"

Ros heard the creak of the massive doors as Darian pried them open. She shuffled back slowly, using Cassian's unlikely distraction to sidle closer to the sanctum. It was only as she reached the safety of the doorway that she realized what strange emotion had overtaken Gilthroy le Fevre. She had pieced it together before through Gaius' words, but with everything else going on, she hadn't been given a chance to tell Cassian the truth that could change everything for him: Gilthroy le Fevre was his father.

"I don't know what they've told you," Cassian said to the Fire house lord burning in front of him. "But your son lives. Florian is safe and working to help the injured. He asked us to secure the sanctum, and that is all we intend to do."

"My son..."

"He's fine," Cassian said.

"You don't understand."

"And there's too much happening to sort it out. Rest assured that our goals are one and the same. We both fight for Fire house."

Cassian's words seemed to hit their mark, and for a second Rosalinde thought Lord le Fevre would extinguish his power and join them. But the moment passed, and Gilthroy ignited his flames to burn hotter than before.

"I will do my best to protect you, son, but I cannot let my house suffer because of my own sentiments. Join me and leave that vile temptress to her fate, or you will burn with her."

A growl erupted from Cassian as he said, "I will not abandon Queen Rosalinde now, or ever again."

Gilthroy nodded. Without a word, he raised his hands as if to send his flames toward Cassian. Rosalinde's hand shot up before he had the chance to act. A tsunami wave of water shot from her, rushing through the courtyard and drenching all in its wake. Unprepared for the onslaught, it extinguished Gilthroy's flames and left him screeching like a drowned cat.

Darian grabbed Cassian's arms and pulled him into the

sanctum. They slammed the doors shut, bolting them from the inside. "We can't hold them off forever," Darian said, his usual playful demeanor gone.

Ros glanced around the sanctum, her mind racing as she took in the room's imposing atmosphere. The walls were lined with towering shelves, each crammed with ancient tomes and scrolls, their leather-bound spines cracked and faded from centuries of use. In the dim light, the titles inscribed in forgotten languages glimmered faintly, hinting at the wealth of knowledge contained within.

The floor was a mosaic of dark stone, worn smooth by the passage of time, yet still bearing intricate patterns that seemed to shift and change as the light played across them. At the room's center stood a massive stone table, its surface etched with runes that pulsed with a faint glow the same color as Gilthroy le Fevre's flames. Scattered across it were various relics and artifacts, each one exuding magic that hummed in the air, vibrating with barely contained power.

In one corner, a pedestal held a crystal orb that glowed with an inner light, casting shifting colors across the room as if it were alive, constantly absorbing and reflecting the magic that filled the space. Nearby, a series of weapons— swords, daggers, and staffs—hung on the walls, their edges sharp and gleaming despite their age, as if waiting for a worthy hand to wield them.

Heavy tapestries hung from the ceiling, depicting scenes of battles, rituals, and ancient rites, their rich colors muted by time but still vivid enough to convey the weight of history they carried. The air was thick with the scent of old parchment, burning incense, and something darker, a burning scent that hinted at the arcane energies permeating every part of the room.

In the far corner, a narrow, spiraling staircase of wrought iron led upwards, disappearing into the shadows above, hinting at further secrets hidden within the depths of the sanctum. The entire space was steeped in an aura of mystery and danger, a place where the past and the present converged, filled with relics of unimaginable power waiting for the right moment—or the right person—to awaken them.

With some effort, Ros tore her eyes from the magical items, reaching for her with unseen threads of magic. She said, "We don't need to hold this place forever. We only have to hold them off long enough for reinforcements."

Cassian said, "Gilthroy le Fevre was the reinforcements."

"He's a good man, but he's been deceived. Hopefully, he'll come to his senses soon and we can help each other. Until then…" she trailed off.

Cassian followed her gaze, understanding dawning in his eyes. "You mean to use the sanctum's magic."

Ros nodded. "It's our only chance. If the relics can create a barrier, that could be enough to give us the upper hand."

Darian looked uncertain. "Are you sure you can control it?"

Ros met his gaze. "I have to try. For Cordelia, for Florian, for all of Fire house."

"It is the very thing the Lord Ruler is trying to avoid; it violates the sanctity of his house for an outsider to use this magic," Cassian said.

"If I could count on Lord le Fevre to be reasonable, I wouldn't consider it. But Florian asked us to protect this place, and it is the only thing I can think to do."

"And it still won't save you."

Ros, Cassian, and Darian turned to the voice. Ahead of them, materializing from the shadows themselves, was Gaius. His dark hair was slicked back from his sallow, haunted face. The sharp features that made Cassian beautiful distorted Gaius into something monstrous. He was marred by the very darkness he sought to control; indeed, it was the dark veins pulsing under his pale skin, the black eyes that spoke of nothing but void, the hatred bubbling out of him in streams of shadows that fizzled into nothingness once they separated from him.

"Brother," Cassian said, voice breaking on the word. He took a step toward him, but Ros grabbed his arm to hold him in place.

Gaius looked at her hand on Cassian's arm and smiled —no, not a smile, but a predator showing his teeth. "Look at that affection, such love between family. I have to admit I feel proud to have brought my brother and sister together, a united front."

Ros cringed at the words. They felt wrong, despite the

truth in them. Had he really brought them together? In a way, maybe, to fight against the evil he presented. But they had found one another before they knew he formed a bridge between them, had moved together of their own accord.

Cassian was taut as a bowstring beside her, tensed and ready for release. Gaius' words had affected him just as they had Ros, but where she could remove herself from the half-brother she barely knew, Cassian still sought love and validation from the person he'd spent years trying to impress.

"He can only speak lies," Ros said. Though her eyes never left Gaius, she could feel Cassian relax ever so slightly beside her.

"Little sister," Gaius said. He placed a hand on his chest as if wounded. "Your opinion of me darkens with each passing day, and yet you've never even attempted to understand things from my point of view. Honestly, I'm offended."

"There's nothing to understand. You are evil, plain and simple."

Gaius tsked. "No one is plain and simple, even if you could somehow understand the motives moving them. As with every other person you've encountered, I contain multitudes. Some dark and 'evil,' as you say, but certainly not all."

"You do give off evil vibes," Darian said.

Gaius slowly turned his gaze to Darian. "This does not concern you." He flicked his hand as if swiping away a bug, and Darian burst into nothingness. Where he had been, motes of dust fluttered to the ground.

A sob erupted from Ros as her hand flew to cover her mouth. She stared at the space where Darian had been and asked, "Why?"

"Why?" Gaius asked, his voice rising. "Why? Because he was nothing. Because he wasted my space, my air, my time. He was powerless to stop me, and so are you."

Gaius pulled the shadows to him then, and at the same moment, Ros pushed Cassian out of his brother's path. In that second, she was prepared to take the full brunt of his power, to accept the oncoming destruction, as long as it meant Cassian would be protected for a moment longer.

But the devastation didn't come.

Ros looked up at the Night mage in front of her, the necromancer who protected her, toyed with her, and wanted her death all within the same breath. Gaius stared at her with unmasked curiosity, and she briefly saw in his eyes the multitude he spoke of.

"You would sacrifice yourself for him?"

"Yes."

"No hesitation?" he asked. "No thoughts about giving up your own power, your own hopes for yourself and this kingdom?"

"If Cassian is gone, there is no hope for me."

"I don't understand," Gaius said, his tone conveying frustrated confusion.

"I love him," Ros said. And though she didn't look at Cassian, she could feel his eyes on her as she said it. "He doesn't know how much—or at least he didn't before this —but I am willing to die for him. If it means he gets to go on and have a beautiful life, one where he can work to make Talabrih better, I will sacrifice myself for him."

Gaius dropped his hands to his side, and for a moment he looked as if he'd given up on his vile plans as he considered Rosalinde's words. When he turned back to her, his eyes seemed strangely sad. "I have never been loved like that."

"You have," Cassian said.

Gaius turned his gaze toward his brother. For the first time since Ros had met the man she knew as darkness, as evil incarnate, he held no malice in his face for Cassian. His contempt was dimmed by whatever else haunted him in that moment.

But Cassian, for the first time in his life, seemed prepared for the hate that didn't come. Cassian's fingers curled around the first of three items: a gleaming silver chain that seemed almost alive in his grasp, slithering slightly as if eager to enact whatever use the long-forgotten mages who had crafted it had designed it for. The links were intricately woven, each one inscribed with tiny runes that shimmered faintly in the low light.

Next, Cassian held aloft a crystalline orb the size of a man's fist. Inside, dark, stormy clouds swirled, trapped within the glassy surface. The swirling turned a deep black as shadows moved from Gaius toward the orb.

"What is this?" Gaius asked. He tried to pull the shadows back to himself, but the orb seemed to absorb his energy.

As he struggled to contain his shadows, the chain in

Cassian's hand somehow elongated as it slid down his arm and across the floor, creeping toward Gaius while he was distracted. It reached his brother's feet and wrapped tightly around them. Gaius cried out in surprise and tried to kick the chain away, but it was too late.

"You never paid attention to our lessons," Cassian said, his tone sad as he reflected on their childhood. "Mother always had much to teach us, about our gifts, about the powers of the past, and about the items in the world that could matter if we chose to let them."

"Brother," Gaius said, his voice pleading. "Don't do this."

"The Bind of Eternus," Cassian continued, "suppresses magical abilities. Even now, you probably feel your power becoming less accessible. The runes draw strength from you, and tighten with every attempt to break free."

Gaius said, "I will leave. I will remove myself and all of my influence from this place and let you recover."

Cassian shook his head. "It's too late for that. The Orb of Nullus is already at work, Gaius. It is an artifact of immense power. It's absorbing your magic as we speak."

"You would do this to me? You would take away everything I've worked for?"

Cassian's gaze moved to Ros for a second before he turned back to his brother. "I will do whatever it takes to protect Rosalinde, and to keep Talabrih from falling to the wickedness you wish to unleash."

"Evil is upon this kingdom, with or without me."

"Without you," Cassian said, swallowing. "We will remove you from the equation and see what is left."

Gaius laughed, a bitter sound. "So much for the love you claim to have for me."

"You squandered that love."

"Conditional love is no love at all."

"You're trying to weaponize my feelings for you, and I won't let it happen," Cas said. "I know how much I ached for your approval, how desperately I wanted a relationship with you, and since I discovered you were alive, how I've longed to save you. But you are beyond saving, no matter what my broken heart wants."

Gaius fell to his knees, the Bind of Eternus fully wrapped around his body now. "You were always a jealous child, a pitiful thing that couldn't keep up with your ambition. Now you see a chance to take away your competition."

"Now I see a way to save the kingdom," Cassian said. "But I will miss you, Gaius. No matter what you think, I do love you. I always have. You have meant more to me than you will ever know."

With those last words, Gaius faded from existence, his body turning to shadow and flowing into the Orb of Nullus. As Ros watched the last of the darkness enter, she could have sworn she saw a hand press against the inside of the orb, then disappear into the storm within. Though his influence would continue until they could reverse the damage he had done, Gaius was no more.

Eight

R os and Cassian moved quickly through the room, gathering the relics and positioning them where they belonged, as many had been pulled from their resting places by the magic Cassian had used. Ros could feel the mystical pull of sorcery thrumming beneath her fingertips as she reached for a sword embedded in the floor. The weapon had somehow fallen from its stand and lodged itself into the marble so that it was standing straight up, calling to anyone who could pry it free.

The sword pulsed with a power that was almost palpable. The blade itself was forged from a metal that seemed to drink in the light—a deep, lustrous silver that shimmered with an ethereal glow. Along its edge, faint runes were etched, their shapes shifting and undulating as if alive and searching for a master to speak its secrets into existence. The hilt was wrapped in black leather, worn smooth from use, yet still exuding an aura of strength and authority.

As the sword was drawn, the atmosphere encompassing it seemed to hum with a low, resonant frequency, vibrating with the arcane energy contained within the weapon. A faint, crackling aura surrounded it, like the shimmer of heat on a hot day, distorting the air and casting off tendrils of light that flickered and danced around it. The light wasn't warm, but cold—sharp and cutting, like the blade itself.

Seizing the hilt was like grasping a lightning bolt frozen in time, the power thrumming beneath the surface, eager to be unleashed. It sent a tingling sensation through Rosalinde's arm, as if the very essence of the weapon was seeking to merge with her soul. The energy radiating from the sword was both intoxicating and overwhelming, a heady mix of raw strength and ancient wisdom, beckoning her to wield it with purpose and resolve.

"I think I need this," she said, her voice full of awe and a covetous desire.

"I'm certain you don't," Cas said.

"You lack the understanding of what we mean to each other," she whispered. "It needs me, too. We were meant to be together."

"Take your hand off the sword," he said.

Ros shook her head. "We could win the war with this. One weapon, one wielder, one end."

"That end is death, Ros. It will turn on you and find a new master."

"It wouldn't do that to me."

"That's what it was made to do," Cassian said. "It

84

destroys everyone who takes it into battle, finding its satisfaction in the collection of blood. It won't help you, it will use you to make itself more powerful."

"Why can't you just be happy for me instead of being jealous?"

"I'm not jealous, love. I'm trying to save you from yourself."

Love. The word reverberated in Rosalinde's mind, shaking her free of the influence the weapon had on her. She looked down at the thing in her hand, her thoughts clear. The sword was more than a weapon—it was a conduit for power that turned the wielder into a living extension of the sword's will. In the hands of a true master, it could shape the course of battles, its power transforming even the simplest swing into an unstoppable force. But she was no true master for the raw and untamed power radiating there. Perhaps no one alive today could wield such a weapon, if anyone ever could have.

Ros put the blade on the shelf in front of her and stepped back. Immediately, the mesmerizing glow faded, and it became a normal sword once more.

She looked up at Cassian, whose gaze was trained on her. There was caution in his stare, and a bit of fear; she wondered what he would have done if she hadn't put the sword down on her own, and how far he would have gone to stop her.

A crash sounded at the door, and the wood splintered under the force of the attackers. Ros closed her eyes, reaching out with her mind to the magic around her. She felt it respond like a living entity that seemed to recognize her desperation.

As the fractured doors burst under the onslaught of the mages outside, Rosalinde's eyes opened, ready to focus on the first person through the door and release her powers. She would do whatever she needed to protect the sanctum and honor her promise to Florian. Ros raised her hands to unleash...

"Stop, please!" Florian yelled. His face was flushed, his golden eyes shining. He had appeared through a passageway behind them, held his hands toward Ros as if begging her to halt, but his eyes darted to the man standing in the doorway in front of them.

Lord Gilthroy le Fevre stood in the ruins of the sanctum door, his shoulders rising and falling with each quick, violent inhale. An aura of fire radiated from him and it clearly took every ounce of control he possessed to stop himself from releasing it to burn through every inch of the chamber, destroying the interlopers.

But then his gaze fell on his son. The heat pouring from him died instantly, and a softness took over as he asked, "Florian?"

"Father?" Florian asked, his voice as broken as his father's had been.

The two men rushed to one another, colliding with a crack that sounded throughout the room. Arms wrapped around his son, Gilthroy said, "They told me you were dead."

"I heard the same of you," Florian said against his shoulder.

"The girl from Water house—"

"She's a friend," Florian said. "She came to protect the sanctum."

Gilthroy's face turned to Ros, though he didn't let go of his son. "I'm sorry for doubting you."

Ros shrugged. "Your home and people were under attack."

"That's no excuse," Gilthroy said.

Florian pulled back and looked his father in the face. "What did you do?"

"I might have been slightly less than cordial."

Ros laughed, unable to stop herself. Gilthroy's words were something his son would say. The men turned to her as they broke apart and she said, "Just barely less."

"Should we prepare for the next wave?" Cassian asked.

"The next... No, no, we're done with fighting," Gilthroy said.

"How?" Ros asked.

"I was planning to ask you that," Gilthroy said, brows raised. "Minutes after you entered the sanctum, the enemy vanished."

Florian repeated, "Vanished?"

Gilthroy nodded. "Everything stopped. The mages flanking the bridges and outside the castle dispersed, the bones in the courtyard evaporated, the flames around Fire house sizzled to nothing. The sounds of battle faded, replaced by the groans and murmurs of the wounded. Smoke still lingers, the acrid scent mingling with the metallic tang of blood, but the only enemy left was in the sanctum."

"The enemy was here," Cassian said. "But not the one you thought."

"Who?" Gilthroy asked, one brow raising.

"My brother, Gaius. He was the one attacking your house."

"Gaius? But he and I were always close. Until…" Gilthroy trailed off, his face contorted as he was lost in memories.

"Nevertheless, he was here, and his power fully controlled the attack. We were able to use the relics in the sanctum to contain him," Cassian said.

"Impossible," Florian said. "The artifacts are keyed to the le Fevre line. Only someone with our ancestral blood could harness their powers."

Gilthroy released the fastens on his armor and stumbled suddenly, falling to his knees. Blood covered the front of his tunic as he looked up into Florian's eyes.

"Father," he croaked. "What's wrong?"

A faint smile crossed Gilthroy's lips as he said, "I gave them hell."

"Healer!" Florian yelled. "Hurry!"

Gilthroy's face was pale, his breathing labored. The once formidable Lord Ruler looked frail, though he'd seemed fine only a moment before.

Cassian joined Florian at Gilthroy's side. He lifted the bloody tunic, revealing a puckered wound with a shadow-black dagger piercing his flesh. Cassian swallowed, his gaze meeting Rosalinde's. He gave her the barest shake of his head. Gilthroy would not make it through this.

"Florian," Gilthroy muttered.

Florian clasped his father's hand, his own voice thick with emotion. "I'm here, Father. You'll be fine."

Gilthroy's eyes, clouded with pain, shone with a different light. "You... you've grown so much over these last months, Florian. I always knew you'd be a great Lord Ruler."

Florian shook his head, struggling to hold back tears. "Don't talk like that. You can overcome this little scratch. We still need you."

But Gilthroy's gaze was already drifting, his strength fading. "I'm proud of you... my son," he murmured. Then, as if remembering something important, his eyes sharpened, and he turned his gaze toward Cassian.

"You," Gilthroy said, his voice gaining a sudden, surprising strength.

Cassian looked up, confusion furrowing his brow. "Yes?"

Gilthroy's eyes softened as he looked at Cassian, a strange mix of sorrow and joy in his expression. "My boy... I never thought I'd get the chance to tell you all the things I need to say, all the things I should have said so very long ago."

Cassian froze, the words not fully registering. "What... what are you talking about?"

Gilthroy smiled weakly, his hand trembling as he

reached out to grasp Cassian's arm. "You... you're my son, too. Your mother and I thought it would protect you if you didn't know. We worried—oh, hells, it doesn't matter now—we were wrong to keep this from you."

Cassian's breath caught in his throat, disbelief and shock washing over him. "What do you mean? How could you be my father?"

Cassian stared at the man who had just revealed the truth, his mind racing to piece together the fragments of his past. The Lord Ruler who had been a distant figure in his life, a man of power and authority, a friend of his mother who visited when he was a child. Until one day he didn't. But this man had never shown him a father's love.

"I don't understand," Cassian stammered, his voice trembling. "Why didn't you ever tell me?"

Gilthroy's eyes filled with tears, his expression one of deep regret. "I wanted to protect you from the burdens of our lineage. I thought you'd be safer if no one knew, not even you. But now I see I was wrong. I should have been there for you, should have told you the truth."

Cassian's emotions swirled in a chaotic storm—anger, hurt, confusion, and a deep sense of loss for the father he never knew he had. "Why now?" he asked, his voice raw. "Why wait until it's too late?"

Gilthroy's grip tightened on Cassian's arm, his strength waning. "I can't go to my grave without telling you. I wanted you to know that I've always loved you, that I've always been proud of you, my son."

Tears welled in Cassian's eyes, blurring his vision as he

looked down at the man who had just shattered everything he thought he knew. He had always wondered about his father, but the reality of it was more painful than he had ever imagined.

"I…" Cassian choked on the words, unable to speak.

Florian, still holding his father's hand, spoke softly. "Cassian, we're brothers. We'll sort through this together."

Gilthroy's breathing grew more labored, and his grip on Cassian's arm weakened. "Take care of each other," he murmured, his voice fading. "And remember my love for you both."

With those final words, Gilthroy's eyes closed, and his body went still. Florian let out a strangled cry, clutching his father's hand as tears streamed down his face. Cassian stood frozen, the reality of the situation crashing down on him with brutal force.

Ros, watching from nearby, felt her heart ache for them both. She moved closer, placing a gentle hand on Cassian's shoulder, offering what comfort she could. "I'm so sorry."

Cassian blinked, the tears finally spilling over as he looked at Ros, his expression one of utter devastation. "He was my father," he said, as if saying the words aloud would make them real. "And now he's gone."

Florian finally let go of his father's hand, his face a mask of grief. "We have to be strong," he said, though his voice trembled. "For him and our people." Florian rubbed a hand over his cheeks, wiping away his tears. "For our sister."

"Our sister," Cassian whispered, the word spoken as if it was from a foreign tongue.

"Cordelia is recovering in safe hands."

Cassian nodded, wiping his eyes with the back of his hand. "We honor him, and we'll protect this kingdom together."

As they stood there, surrounded by the wounded and the dying, Ros knew that this moment would mark a turning point for all of them. The battle had taken much from them, but it had also given them something new—an unbreakable bond forged in the fires of war and loss.

And as they prepared to face whatever came next, they knew they would do it as a family, united by the love and sacrifice of the man who had just left them.

△

THE MORNING AFTER THE BATTLE, Fire house was eerily quiet. The once bustling stronghold now felt like a tomb, its halls filled with the ghosts of the fallen and the memories of a hard-won victory. But there was no time to linger in grief. The kingdom was still in peril, and they needed allies if they were to have any hope of surviving what was to come.

Ros stood by one of the shattered windows, looking out at the charred landscape that surrounded Fire house. Smoke still rose from the ruins of the outer buildings, a grim reminder of the devastation they had barely escaped. She clenched her fists, determination hardening her resolve. They couldn't afford to be caught off guard again. With Gaius contained within the Orb of Nullus, perhaps they would finally have a chance to breathe and to make things right.

Behind her, the others were gathered in the Lord Ruler's study, their expressions mirroring her own mixture of weariness and resolve. Florian had called together a handful of people to discuss their plans; some Ros knew, but several she did not. He'd introduced them to one another, starting with Ros, Cassian, and King Tancred, as well as Sloane, the Healer they'd met when they brought Cordelia home. In addition to them, there was a young woman named Kaith who looked to be near their age, maybe a few years older. Her hair was a brilliant copper color, pulled back into a long braid, and she had the most piercing blue eyes Ros had ever seen. Beside her was Royce le Fevre, one of Florian's uncles, and his husband, Iwan. Both were powerful mages in their prime, but those years had long passed and they were comfortably in the roles as advisors to Fire house.

A heavy silence lingered between them. Though they were all allies to Florian, there was still unease after what had happened the night before.

Cassian, still reeling from the revelation of his father's identity, was the first to break the silence. "We can't stay here," he said, his voice firm despite the lingering sadness in his eyes. "Gaius is gone, but he has allies. They'll soon know where we are if they don't already, and we will not put your people through this again. They've lost too much."

Florian nodded, his expression grave. "You're right. We need to find allies, people who can help us rebuild our strength and take the fight to them before they can strike again."

Ros frowned when she thought of something Darian said. She'd barely known the rogue, but she missed the casual ease he lived in, and she wished he were here right now to lighten the mood. "Darian mentioned some whispers he had heard about a group of rebels gathering in the north, near the old borderlands. He said they're good people, fed up with the madness the throne has brought, ready to fight back. And they're looking for someone to lead them."

Tancred turned to her, curiosity piqued. "How did he know about them?"

She shrugged. "I didn't get to question him about it. But the little time we spent with Darian leads me to believe he was probably one of them, or he wanted to be."

"Word travels fast in the shadows," Sloane said, moving into the room from her position standing against the doorframe. "I've heard about them, too."

"Do you get a lot of information from the shadows?" Cas asked, eyeing her.

Sloane pursed her lips. "I listen to any information I can get my hands on. You never know when it will come in handy."

"Fair," Cassian said. "What do you know about them?"

"They're not just a ragtag gang without resources. They've got weapons, supplies, and most importantly, they've got fire in their hearts. They believe in something better, something worth fighting for."

Ros's eyes narrowed in thought. "They have all that, but not a leader?"

Sloane nodded. "From what I've heard, there is a magicless man with ties to the nobles who has been organizing them, but they're looking for someone to inspire them. If they knew what you've done, how you've stood up against the darkness and the things that are wrong in Talabrih, they would follow you. Are you willing to lead them?"

Ros felt a surge of emotion—pride, fear, and a deep sense of responsibility. The thought of leading a group of rebels was daunting, but she knew she couldn't shy away from it. Too much was at stake.

Florian stepped forward, his hand resting reassuringly on Ros's shoulder. "If they're gathering in the north, we should go to them. But we can't just show up empty-handed. We need to bring them something—hope, a plan, a reason to believe that we can win."

Ros nodded, her mind already racing with possibilities. "We'll take what resources we have left, rally any of your troops that you can spare, and head north. If these rebels will fight, we can give them a cause worth fighting for."

Cassian said, "And if they're willing to follow you, Ros, then we'll have a real chance of turning the tide."

"Trust the Rising Tide," Ros muttered.

"Indeed," Kaith whispered, her voice so soft that Ros wasn't positive she hadn't imagined it.

Rosalinde's thoughts flitted to Alaric. He'd spoken to her about the Tide, promising that there was a rebellion ready to fight when she was ready to lead them. Maybe they were part of the same group he had organized. Maybe that was a sign that he was alive.

"Pack your supplies," Florian said, nodding to Sloane.

"Lord le Fevre," she said, her forehead creasing with the heaviness those words brought. "I will take them north on your behalf, but you're needed here."

"So are you," Dryden said. He had changed from his borrowed guard uniform, but had cleaned up and changed into clothes befitting his station. Despite the beautifully crafted clothing in shades of red, orange, and gold, Dryden no longer looked like a foppish nobleman. There was a look in his eyes that said he had seen more in the last day than he'd ever imagined for a life like his. He would not, could not, go back to the way he had lived before.

"Cousin," Florian breathed, visibly relaxing at seeing Dryden well.

"I knew you'd be up for this," Dryden said. "But you need to be here to help our people rebuild. They'll look to you in this time while they're afraid. And there are still too many injured for Sloane to leave."

"Our people will understand my absence," Florian said.

"Don't ask them to understand. Not when you have another option," Royce said, speaking up for the first time in an effort to protect his young, inexperienced nephew, and the new Lord Ruler.

"What are you suggesting?" Florian asked.

Dryden gave his cousin a grim smile and said, "Send me."

"You don't know what you're asking," Sloane said.

"I'm asking to be of use to my house, to my Lord. No, I am not a warrior, I am not a skilled swordsman, and I'm not known for my charm. I have little to offer the rebels, except the sincere desire to see our kingdom righted."

Ros said, "That's all you need to give."

"You're sure about this?" Florian asked.

Dryden nodded. "I've never been more sure of anything in my life."

"Then you shall be my representative," Florian said.

"Good. Let's go find these rebels and show them what we're made of."

Tancred, who had been quiet until now, finally spoke. "We'll need to move quickly and quietly. Our enemies won't stop until they've crushed every spark of resistance. We need to make sure that spark turns into a wildfire."

Ros looked at her father, took a deep breath, and said the thing she dreaded saying: "I think you should stay here." The king blinked in surprise, clearly taken aback. Ros pressed on, saying, "For the same reason Sloane is staying behind. There are far too many injured, and anyone with the ability to heal should be here."

Her reasoning was sound, and mostly true. She wanted him to stay and help, but she also knew her mind would rest easier knowing he was somewhere safe. Florian and the Fire house mages would take care of him, protect him like their own. Meanwhile, she would traipse through the wilderness to recruit the people who might not fully trust him.

King Tancred nodded, saying, "You're right, of course. I'm needed here, and here I shall remain."

With that settled, Ros looked around at her friends, at those who had stood by her through everything. They had lost so much, but they had also gained something precious —each other. Together, they could take on whatever came their way.

"Let's prepare to leave," she said. "We'll gather what we can, say our goodbyes, and head north. If there's a chance to gather more allies, we can't waste it."

As they moved to make preparations, Ros took one last look through the broken window at the horizon. The future was uncertain, but she knew one thing for sure: they couldn't stay here. The battle for Fire house was over, but the war for the kingdom was just beginning.

They were heading into the unknown, but they were not alone. And somewhere in the north, a group of rebels was waiting—waiting for a leader, waiting for hope. Ros was determined to be both.

Nine

The journey north was grueling. The land they traversed was mostly covered in mountainous terrain, surrounded at other points by impenetrable forests and raging water. There were a handful of villages that had once dotted the land, but were now in ruins, overgrown by vines and wild flora. Their once fertile fields were reduced to barren stretches of dirt or overgrown plants where their crops would have been. Ros didn't know what had led these villages to be abandoned, nor how long they had sat empty.

Cassian scouted ahead as best he could without knowing the area. He shadow-walked to places he could see from a distance, and attempted to plot a course for the rest of the group. In the end, Florian had only been able to give them two dozen guards, in addition to a handful of villagers who had lost everything and wanted to get revenge. There was still too much unknown, and he couldn't leave Fire house completely defenseless.

Having Dryden with them was a boon. The people of Fire house had seen the nobleman don the armor of a guard and fight at their side. Their respect for him had grown drastically by that action, and his presence was sought by every Fire house eye as they traveled. Whatever Dryden said, they agreed. He could have jumped headfirst into the raging whitewaters and they would have followed without question.

Ros and Cassian did their best to keep their group moving swiftly and silently, avoiding the remains of the roads when they could. Though there weren't any people around that they could see, they still set up camp in the most secluded spots they could find, always on edge, always ready to fight if necessary.

Kaith was the most helpful in leading the way, her knowledge of the back roads and hidden paths invaluable. She directed Cassian on the best spots to view and observe their surroundings, and helped him plan their course upon his return. Though she had said little in the meeting where they had been introduced, Ros had gleaned that she was one of Fire house's many spies. Every house had them, but Ros had never met one of them who was so open about what they did. Once they had established their plan to go north, Kaith had volunteered quite a bit more information about the rebels that she had been keeping close to herself until she knew how things would play out.

The young woman moved through the shadows with

the ease of someone who had spent most of her life navigating them, a small smirk often playing on her lips as she effortlessly found the safest routes. She was invaluable as a guide, and though she was quiet and serious, there was something playful in her demeanor that found its way to the surface at the strangest times. Had it not been clarified that she was a daughter of Fire house, Ros would have thought she fit right in with Cassian's Night house brood.

"Not much further now," Kaith murmured one evening as they gathered around the meager warmth of their campfire. Her gaze flicked to Ros. "If Alaric is leading these rebels, they'll be well-hidden. He's not one to leave anything to chance."

Ros stiffened at the mention of him, memories flooding back with an intensity she hadn't expected. Alaric. The name alone sent a shiver down her spine. He had been her everything once—a friend, a confidant, a lover. But that felt like years ago, before the world had torn them apart. She had thought him lost after what had happened at Earth house, swallowed by the chaos that had consumed the kingdom. And now, to hear that he was not only alive but leading a group of rebels...

Cassian noticed the change in her expression and frowned. He turned to Kaith and asked, "You're certain the rebel leader's name is Alaric?"

She nodded. "You know him?"

"Maybe," Cas said.

"Brown hair, hazel eyes, scar above his left eye," she said. "Handsome devil, and damn good with a blade."

"He spent his life around swords. Alaric was a black-smith before all of this," Ros whispered.

"Ah, you do know him, then."

Ros hesitated, then nodded. "We were close once. Before..." Her voice trailed off as she stared into the flickering flames. "I wasn't sure he was still alive."

The others exchanged glances, sensing the weight of the revelation. Dryden placed a hand on her shoulder. "If he's leading these rebels, that's a good sign. He must be someone they trust. We can use your connection to get their attention when we arrive."

Ros nodded, though her mind reeled. She couldn't afford to stay lost in the past, or worried about the things that had pushed her and Alaric apart. There was too much at stake to wonder whether their split had left him in a place where they could work together, or if he would prefer to give her a wide berth. They were on the brink of something important, something that could turn the tide of this war.

THE NEXT MORNING, they broke camp early, their pace quickening as they neared the old borderlands. The terrain became rocky and rough, the air colder. Kaith led them through a narrow pass between jagged hills, the ground littered with fallen rocks and debris. The path was treacherous, but it offered them cover—anyone following would have a hard time staying unnoticed.

By midday, they reached the narrow mouth of a valley. It opened between two of the tallest mountains Ros had ever seen. Though she couldn't see much of the area ahead through the tapered gap, what she could see was lush compared to the barren land they had crossed, with dense trees and vegetation on either side.

Kaith held up a hand, signaling for them to stop. She said, "This is it. If the rebels are here, and all my intel suggests this is where they've made their base, they'll be hidden in this valley. We should move carefully from here on out."

"The entrance is a chokehold," Cassian said. "Beneficial for them if someone is trying to get in, but less so if their forces need to escape. Is there another way out?"

Kaith gave a noncommittal shrug. Not for the first time, Ros wondered how connected the Fire house spy truly was with this rebel group.

Ros motioned for Dryden, understanding that the people from Fire house were devoted to his every desire and that she would get things done easier by using that to her advantage. She pointed to the valley's entrance and said, "We're going through there. We know the rebels are here, but not exactly where. Can you get your people to pair up and move as quietly as possible?"

Dryden's face shifted into a look of confusion. "I'll do anything you ask, my queen, but why have me speak to them when you could do it?"

Ros gave him a small smile. "They know you, and they trust you. I'm only an ideal to them."

"Sometimes that's what people need."

"Maybe to get them started, but everyone craves comfort and stability. They have that with you. It makes it easier for them to fall into whatever line you draw for them."

Dryden shrugged. "I'll talk to them, of course. Just don't ignore the power you have. The people want someone to believe in, and they see the work you're doing to make yourself a genuine friend of every citizen in Talabrih."

Ros nodded, her heart pounding in her chest. Dryden's words rang of truth, but she wasn't at a point where she could fully think about them. Once they found the rebels and made plans, maybe she could feel secure enough in what they were doing to take control. Ros hoped so, because she was counting on her persuasiveness to move them to action.

She motioned for the others to find their positions, keeping low as they advanced into the valley. The tension in the air was palpable, every rustle of leaves and snap of twigs making them jump.

After what felt like hours of creeping through the forest, they finally came upon a clearing. It was well-hidden, surrounded by towering trees and thick under-brush. In the center, a large group of people was gathered —men and women of all ages, armed and armored, their faces set with determination.

At the head of the group stood a tall figure, his back to them. Even from a distance, Ros recognized him. Alaric.

Her breath caught in her throat as she took in the sight of him; his presence was commanding, his powerful body erupting with energy and motion as he gave instructions to the assembly. Ros watched his movements, her mind transfixed on how much he had changed in such a short time. Or, more likely, she had never fully known the man in front of her and all he was capable of while they were slinking around for a bit of mutual satisfaction.

Beside Ros, Kaith cleared her throat. Alaric looked up at the sound, a smile blooming across his face. Ros returned the smile tentatively, her body seeming to relax for the first time in days. Still, she wasn't sure what to do now that the rebel leader was in front of her.

Kaith, catching Rosalinde's hesitation, gave her a gentle nudge. "Go on," she whispered. "They're waiting for you."

Ros took a deep breath, steeling herself, and stepped forward. The murmur of conversation died down as the rebels noticed her and the others approaching. For a moment, the world seemed to stand still. Ros could see the flicker in his eyes, the way his breath hitched slightly, and she knew he was thinking of all they had been to one another, just as she had been the moment before.

"Ros," he said once she was in earshot, his voice rich and deep. "I knew you'd find us eventually. Took longer than I expected, if I'm being honest."

She swallowed hard, forcing herself to stay composed. "When I climbed up through the Rocks of Maldrith to search for a band of rebels to join my cause, I didn't expect to find you here."

He stepped forward, closing the distance between them. "Where else would I be?"

"Finding somewhere safe to live out your days?" she asked.

Alaric shook his head. "We're well past that. There is no chance for peace unless we earn it."

"You shouldn't have to earn peace," Ros said.

Alaric shrugged. "Maybe not, but you and I both know that's where we are."

"And you're all willing to fight for it?"

Alaric nodded. "We are. What about you?"

Ros took a deep breath and slowly released it. With a nod, she said, "I am."

"Good. Because we've been waiting for you. When we heard what you'd done—how you stood against the traitors trying to usurp the throne—we knew you were the key."

"I'm nothing without the people of Talabrih," Ros said. "And all I want is to protect and help them."

"I know. We know. And we want the same thing."

Ros felt a swell of emotions—relief, hope, and the bittersweet sting of the past. "That's why I came looking for the Rising Tide. We need your help. The kingdom is on the brink of collapse. If we don't unite, everything we've fought for will be lost."

Alaric's expression grew serious, his gaze sweeping over the others. "We're with you, Rosa. All of us. We've been gathering strength, waiting for the right moment to strike back. With you leading us, we have that moment."

The rebels murmured in agreement, their eyes filled

with trust and hope. Ros felt the weight of their expectations, but she also felt something else—a renewed sense of purpose.

"Then let's not waste any time," she said, her voice strong. "We have a kingdom to save."

Alaric nodded, his eyes locked on hers. "Together."

As the rebels prepared for their next move, Ros allowed herself a small smile. They had found their allies. And with Alaric by her side once more, she knew they were ready to face whatever came next.

But even as she felt the warmth of hope returning, there was an unspoken tension between her and Alaric that still had not dissipated despite all that had happened—a lingering question of what had been lost, and if it could be regained.

Her eyes slid to Cassian for only a second. He was quietly watching, letting things play out as they needed to. Though he had a jealous streak, especially where Alaric was concerned, Ros knew he would do nothing to endanger the work they were doing with the rebels. Even if he had to fight tooth and nail to hold back his emotions for the greater good.

That situation, she knew, would have to wait. She couldn't face her past with Alaric and her future with Cassian while they were in the middle of saving Talabrih. For now, they had a war to win.

Ten

The rebel camp bustled with activity as Ros, Alaric, and the others gathered in the heart of the clearing. Makeshift tables were strewn with maps, diagrams, and scattered notes—plans hastily drawn for their plight of taking back the kingdom. The mood was tense, the air thick with the weight of what they were about to undertake.

Ros stood at the head of the table, her fingers tracing the worn edges of a map that detailed the layout of Water house. There were some issues with the map, parts incomplete that an outsider wouldn't know. It was clear to Ros that Alaric had used his time coming to her room well, and that details of his visits were included in the survey. There were certain parts—like the broom closet where they'd hidden for far longer than it took to avoid the guards making their rounds, or the secret passages the royals used to move their lovers in and out of the castle—that were intricately detailed. Other portions of Water house, though more public, were left blank.

As the holder of the crown for decades and the house most centrally located in Talabrih, the stronghold was strategically vital. Its location was only part of it; Water house was most desirable to Ros because of who was inside. Her sister, Elsabet, was there, as was their mother; the uncertainty of their loyalties gnawed at Rosalinde's heart, especially after her last encounter with her mother, where Gaius had used her to attack Ros.

She closed her eyes and took a deep breath, letting her worries out with her exhale. Ros couldn't afford to think about those things right now. First, they had to get to Water house.

"We'll need to approach from the east," Ros said, her voice steady but tinged with a tension she couldn't entirely hide. "The terrain there is rougher, but it offers more cover. We can get close before they even know we're there."

Alaric nodded, his brow furrowed as he studied the map. "We can split into two groups. One will create a diversion at the main gate, drawing their forces out. The second group, led by you, Ros, will slip in through the eastern side and take the inner courtyard. From there, we'll have to fight our way to the heart of Water house."

Cassian leaned forward, his expression grim. "Do we know how many men they have inside?"

Kaith, who had been spying the area for weeks, spoke up. "They've got at least a hundred, maybe more. And they're well-fortified. But their leadership is shaky—their new rulers haven't exactly earned loyalty. We might be able to turn some of their men against them if we play it right."

Ros's heart sank as she considered the odds. They were outnumbered, and even with the element of surprise, this would be a bloody fight.

"I cannot bear this conversation without offering a suggestion that we try negotiation first," Cassian said.

"Those in control will not accept any terms. They want to control this kingdom, and they will do whatever it takes to do so," Alaric said.

Cassian smacked his fist on the table. "These are our people, dammit. Just like my people at Night house in the wars before us, the men and women at Water house are being used—they didn't sign up for this—and forcibly removing them from our path, to murder them for doing the jobs assigned to them... I will not stand for it."

Alaric leaned forward, his glare meeting that of Cassian's. Ros had seen lesser men bow and snivel in the presence of the heir to Night house, but the blacksmith-turned-rebel stood his ground. "The nobles have fostered a kingdom where people are denigrated for a lack of magic, where they are belittled, cast out, and harmed for something they cannot control. Now that the magicless are stepping up to take back their home, you think you can decide how they do it?"

"I didn't create this kingdom," Cassian said. "I want change just as much as you do, but the traditions of the past are rooted in the people here. It takes time to alter the course."

"And you, with the power to change that, did nothing. You might not have instilled those values in the mages across the kingdom, but you also didn't discourage it."

"I'm one man, in a house disregarded for an age. I've tried to make small changes—"

"Not good enough," Alaric said.

"Just admit what this is really about, Alaric. You're furious that Rosalinde chose me over you. Every word you speak is tainted by your hatred of me."

Alaric's cheeks flushed as he balled his fists at his side. "Rosa didn't choose you over me, you dolt; she accepted her duty to her kingdom as it was presented to her. There was no room for me in that version of her life."

"And you think taking over a group of misfits and rabble rousers will change that?"

Alaric growled. "These people have more fire in the bones, more sense in their heads, and more love and kindness in their hearts than you could possibly understand."

"Damn right we do," one of Alaric's men said.

Alaric smiled and nodded toward his people, pride clear on his face. Ros had never seen the fire burning in Alaric like it did now as he spoke to Cassian, despite years of time with him, of caring more deeply about him than she had anyone before, to the point that she thought she could have loved him if not for whatever connection bonded her and Cassian. Alaric had found something with these rebels, something that was missing from his former life, and Ros was glad there was finally something to stoke the ember of his heart into a flame.

Cassian smiled at Alaric then, and Rosalinde's heart seized with the realization of what he'd just done. Cassian had allowed their conversation to turn him into a villain to show them who their leader was and how he believed in them. Alaric's words would spread through the camp, buoying the spirits of all those preparing to fight. It wouldn't win any favors for Cassian, but they would fight even harder to prove the Night mage wrong.

"Damn right they do," he said, eyes staring straight into Alaric's. "And they have a leader who understands that, and who will stand up for them no matter the cost."

Alaric's eyes narrowed as if he suspected what Cassian was doing, but wasn't convinced. He asked, "So, what, we're just supposed to trust you're on our side?"

"I honestly do not care what you believe," Cassian replied. "I have been doubted and mistrusted my entire life because I was born with the ability to mold shadows. The strange thing is, when no one believes in you, every day you decide to believe in yourself. I know who I am, Alaric, and I know what I'm about. You aren't the only one who will do whatever it takes to make things right for these people."

"I believe him," a voice said from the doorway.

Ros watched as a figure with short black hair walked through the parting assembly. Though the people gathered for the planning meeting were the strongest of both Alaric's and Dryden's forces, they still moved out of the way like a herd of deer dispersing in front of a stalking hellcat. And maybe that's what she was. For as she came into view and Ros saw the owner of that voice, she felt a jolt in her gut that made her want to run like the rest of them.

Brisa Delos Santos was not an imposing figure in stature, but she carried herself with the authority and confidence that only someone of her heritage could. As the last of the royal family that had been in power long before Rosalinde's family had been on the throne, Brisa was the *almost* queen. She could have taken her rightful place if she wished for it—mages and magicless alike would surely crown her for her name alone—but she didn't want it. Though she had vowed to take power if it was the only way, her goal was to help an ally end up in charge.

"Brisa," Cassian said, her name turning into a relaxed sigh on his lips. He opened his arms, and she moved toward his embrace. "I'm so glad you're alive."

She laughed as she said, "Me, too. And it's good to see you as well, Lord Cassian."

"None of that. You know better than to start with all of that 'lord' stuff," he said.

Brisa pulled back and looked at him. Quietly, she said, "I know you don't like it, but it's still nice for the others to hear. They need that if they're going to trust you."

"They aren't," he said. "And I'm fine with that. They need to trust our queen."

Brisa and Cassian both looked at Ros then, who had silently taken in their display. She had never fully understood the relationship between them. They had both called the other "friend," and maybe that was truly all there was between them, like her and Florian. But it was clear from

Rosalinde's previous interactions with the girl that she was willing to do anything Cassian asked, including endangering herself. Was that the mark of a deep friendship, or something more?

"Rosa?" Alaric said, tearing into her thoughts.

"Yes?"

"What is your answer? How do you want to enter Water house?"

"I will not allow us to kill anyone we don't have to," Ros said, looking between her future companion and her former lover. "There are surely some at Water house who will welcome us."

"And we're supposed to guess at who they are?" Alaric asked.

"I can help with that."

Ros turned to the voice, her heart jumping with excitement when she saw Romenia standing there. She had always been Rosalinde's favorite guard at Water house and had committed to help her even when it meant giving up her position and all she'd worked for. The woman had always been impeccably clean, her armor buffed and shining; now, she was covered in a layer of dirt, and her braided hair held a greasy sheen. Ros had last seen her bloodied and bruised at Earth house, but all that was left of that now was a thin pink scar at her temple. She was an imposing figure, a fighter through and through, and Ros was relieved to see her here in one piece.

"You should be on patrol," Alaric said.

Romenia nodded her head toward him and said, "I

respect your position as a leader in this rebellion, and I have never questioned your commands, even when they did not use my strengths effectively. But if you think I'm going to patrol these deserted woods while my queen stands here making battle plans and needing my help, you're out of your head."

Alaric put his hands on his hips and said, "We patrol for a reason. You know that."

"Right, and you know you could send anyone to do that job. There are ten men milling about the camp with nothing to do at this very moment. Send one of them—hells, send all of them, I don't care. My place is at Queen Rosalinde's side."

There was an awkward silence for a second before Dryden smiled broadly at Romenia and said, "I get it now."

Everyone turned to Dryden, who held his hands up in surrender. Romenia said, "Get what?"

"My cousin's obsession with you. He only just met you but hasn't stopped going on about you."

Romenia's brows furrowed. "Cousin?"

"Apologies," he said. "I am Dryden le Fevre, cousin to the Lord Ruler of Fire house, Florian le Fevre."

Romenia blinked as if the name had smacked her, and she was struggling to gain her senses. Finally, she whispered, "Florian? He lives?"

Dryden nodded, and Romenia's face broke out into a grin that changed everything about her. Romenia's large stature had been the thing Ros had noticed first, followed by her long blonde braid. Looking at her now, Ros took in the sight of a beautiful woman. Her loyalty and heart had always shone through—her love for the royal family and her dedication to her kingdom were the sorts of things bards wrote songs about—but Romenia displayed those things without drawing attention to how lovely she was. Or maybe it was just the knowledge that Florian was whole and hale that made her glow.

"Not to distract from the joyful news," Cassian said, tapping the map, "but we need to sort this out. How can you help us with the guards?"

Romenia wiped the smile from her face and tried to school herself into something more neutral. She stepped closer to the rest of the group and said, "I've worked with those guards for years. They know me, and they know what I'm about. If I go to them first, they'll listen."

"We had to break Rosa out of Water house the last time we were there, and there were not a lot of guards supporting the cause," Alaric said.

"They didn't understand what was happening. There was too much chatter from everyone else, and too many people giving orders that made little sense. They took the easiest path."

"You're certain you can change that?" Ros asked.

"I am."

"Without endangering yourself?"

Romenia stared at her queen and gave a shrug. "There is danger. I won't make myself a liar by saying otherwise. But it is worth the risk if we can save some of them."

Ros nodded. She bit her lip, hating what she was about

to say, but saying it anyway. "I agree. I don't like putting you in this position, but I appreciate what you want to do, and I believe we have to try."

If they could take back Water house, they could break the traitors' hold on the region and give their rebellion the stronghold it desperately needed. From there, they had the chance to embark on their own mission and take the fight to Air house to defeat Graeme and anyone else who got in their way.

"There's one more thing," Ros said, her voice dropping as she addressed the elephant in the room. "My sister and mother are at Water house. I want to believe they're innocent in all this, but with everything that has happened, I don't know for sure. If they're aligned with those who oppose us..." She trailed off, unable to finish the thought. The idea of having to face her own sister as an enemy was too painful to fully comprehend. "I've known them my whole life. I want to believe that there is nothing that could have turned them away from goodness, and that they'll fight alongside us for what's right."

"Thirst for power can change people," Alaric said.

Romenia shook her head. "She was the queen. She could do whatever she wished. If she has done something out of character, I'm certain it was for a reason that she'll explain when we have the chance. Sariyah is a champion of the people; she would never harm them."

Brisa, who had been silent until now, spoke up. Ignoring what Romenia said about Sariyah, she instead spoke about the princess. "We must proceed carefully. If

Elsabet is on our side—and I think she is—we'll need to find a way to get her out without tipping off the traitors. If she's not..."

Ros looked up at the former royal family's heir, unsure what to expect from the girl. Rosalinde's eyes pleaded for any sign of reassurance, but there was none to give. Brisa dealt in absolutes; she might hope Elsabet was loyal to Rosalinde, but would be prepared if she was not.

"If she's not," Ros said, swallowing, "then we'll deal with her when the time comes."

Alaric reached out, gently squeezing Rosalinde's hand. "We'll do everything we can to bring her back safely, Rosa. But you need to be ready for whatever we find."

She nodded, trying to steel herself for the possibility that Elsabet might not be the sister she remembered. It was a cold, harsh reality, but she knew she had to face it.

"Right," she said, straightening her shoulders. "We'll stick to the plan. Diversion at the gate, infiltration from the east. We take the inner courtyard and push our way to the keep. Romenia will work from the inside, swaying as many to our side as she can safely do. If we can take down the head of the beast, the rest will fall apart."

"I'll need a few days," Romenia said.

"We can give you two," Alaric replied. "You'll leave when we're finished here."

Romenia looked at Alaric, then turned to Rosalinde. When Ros nodded her agreement, Romenia said, "As you wish."

"I can shadow-walk you to Water house. To the city

outside, at least. That may give you a little more time," Cassian offered.

"Thank you," Romenia said.

Ros spoke up. "We'll need to move quickly once we're inside. The longer we linger, the more likely they are to regroup. And we can't afford to get bogged down in the outer levels. Our target is the internal rooms where they'll be holed up."

Alaric tapped the map with the hilt of his sword. "We can send a small team ahead to disable anyone who might sound the alarm. If we can take out their signalers before the main attack, they won't be able to call for reinforcements."

Kaith grinned, already volunteering. "I'll take care of that. I've got a few tricks up my sleeve."

Ros nodded, grateful for her confidence. "Good. And once we've taken the courtyard, we'll signal the rest of the rebel forces. They'll be in place to storm the gates once we're in position."

The room fell into a tense silence as everyone absorbed the plan. It was risky, but it was their best chance.

Ros looked around at the faces of her companions—each one determined, ready to follow her into the fray. She felt a surge of pride mixed with fear. They were risking everything for this, for her, and for a chance to take back their kingdom.

"Get some rest," she finally said, breaking the silence. "We move at dawn. And remember—this isn't just about taking back Water house. It's about taking back our future."

As the others dispersed to make final preparations, Cassian and Alaric lingered. Ros looked between Alaric and Cassian, the two men dedicated to fighting by her side to save this kingdom. She gave Cassian a tight-lipped smile and said, "Go help Romenia."

"You're alright?" he asked.

She nodded. "I'm worried, but it's a good plan."

He put his hand on her shoulder and said, "We're going to do this. You'll have Talabrih back, and then the real work can begin."

He gave Alaric a terse nod before leaving to help Romenia find her way to Water house.

Ros turned to Alaric then, unsure what to say. They had shared so much over the years. The relationship that had once seemed so powerfully overwhelming to her, so massively important, now felt like a fever dream. She still cared for Alaric, but it was in a way she had never imagined for them.

Alaric's eyes searched hers. "Rosa," he said quietly, "no matter what happens, we'll face it together. I won't let you do this alone. I will make sure you are safe, that you end up on the throne in the end."

"Thank you, Alaric. I'm glad you're here."

He smiled softly, and with a tentative tone, he said, "I understand things are different with us. I'm not doing this because I want you back, or because I'm hoping you'll see me differently. This is something I truly believe in, and something I'm willing to fight for. I'm healing, Rosa, and the rebels are helping me do that."

"I know," she said. "I can see it."

"You've changed, too. It's obvious in the way you speak, the way you carry yourself. You were always questioning yourself, but now there's a surety in the decisions you make. People respond to it."

"I just hope I'm making the right decisions."

Alaric nodded. "You are making the best choices you can, considering all the unknown, and trying to plan a way around it. It won't be a perfect plan—there's no such thing —but it's as good as we could hope for."

Ros nodded, acknowledging his words despite the worry twisting in her gut. She hoped he was right. The time for planning was over, and they would enact the one they had, even though there were risks. Now it was time to fight.

Eleven

The first sight of Water house filled the rebels with a tense mix of dread and determination. Outside of the castle walls was the main town, where artisans and merchants had shops to support local residents and visitors to Water house. There were homes there, families, and Ros wanted to avoid their involvement at all cost. She had lovely memories of that town and the people who lived there, and she refused to tarnish the city with the imminent battle.

The stronghold stood like a dark sentinel against the early morning light, its towering walls casting long shadows over the landscape and the town below it. Once a place of safety and refuge, it now loomed as a fortress of treachery, its battlements lined with soldiers.

Ros led the group through the thick underbrush that surrounded the eastern side of the stronghold. Every step was measured, every breath held as they approached the outer perimeter. Behind her, the rebels moved in near silence, their faces set with grim resolve. Kaith and her team had already gone ahead to disable the soldiers who would raise the alarm; they were counting on her success to ensure that no reinforcements could be summoned.

Alaric, moving close beside Ros, gave her a reassuring nod as they reached the edge of the forest. "This is it," he whispered, his voice barely audible. "We move quickly and quietly. Once we're inside, we don't stop until we've taken the inner courtyard."

Ros's heart pounded in her chest, but she forced herself to stay calm. The plan was simple, but its execution would be anything but. The weight of the weapon grounded her in the moment as she tightened her grip on the hilt of the sword Alaric had given her. She had never been particularly gifted with weapons, but there was no room for fear now—only action. She couldn't risk using her magic until they were in the thick of things or she could tip off the guards to their presence. Though Ros had grown in her gifts since she'd been away from Water house, she still lacked subtlety and was more brute force than precision.

With a quick signal from Ros, the rebels moved out of the trees, darting across the open ground that separated them from the walls of Water house. The eastern side was less guarded because of the difficult landscape, just as they'd hoped, but a few sentries still patrolled the area. Kaith's team had taken down most of the watchtowers, but they couldn't risk drawing attention too soon. Finished with their initial task, they were hidden and waiting, ready to aim their bows as soon as Ros gave the signal.

As they reached the base of the wall, Alaric took the lead, using a grappling hook to scale the rough stone. It was a sight to behold, his movements swift and precise, and within moments he was perched on the battlements, signaling for the others to follow. One by one, the rebels ascended; if they were anything like Ros as she climbed the wall, their veins thrummed with the adrenaline of impending battle, the sound of their beating hearts blocking out all other thoughts.

Once they were all on the wall, Ros took a moment to orient herself. Below them lay the inner courtyard, where dozens of armed guards were stationed. There were very few that she recognized from Water house, but there were many in Air and Earth house colors. How had Graeme and Gaius convinced so many to turn against the throne? And what was going on inside Water house that would convince them to let other houses show force within their walls?

Ros could see the soldiers moving about, unaware of the danger creeping up on them. The outdoor space was filled with them, but their attention was focused on the main gate, where Dryden's diversionary force would soon strike.

"Stay low," Ros murmured, leading the way along the battlements. "We take out the sentries first, then we hit the courtyard with everything we have."

The rebels moved with deadly efficiency, dispatching the few sentries they encountered with silent precision.

Ros could feel the tension building as they neared the point of no return. Everything hinged on this moment.

As they reached the top of a stairwell leading down into the courtyard, Ros signaled for Alaric's people to take their positions. Cassian, Brisa, and a few others prepared to descend. The plan was to strike hard and fast, using the element of surprise to create chaos among the enemy ranks.

Ros glanced at Alaric, who was watching her closely. "We need to move now," she said, her voice firm.

Alaric nodded, then turned to the rebels. "Remember, this is for our future. For every person who's suffered under a life of unjust decisions and unbalanced rule. For every life lost in the pursuit of equity. We take back Talabrih today!"

They murmured their agreement, their resolve solidified. With one last look at the courtyard below, Ros gave the signal.

The first arrow flew from Kaith's bow, striking an Air house guard in the throat. He fell without a sound, and for a heartbeat, the world seemed to hold its breath. Then, all at once, chaos erupted.

The rebels erupted out of the stairwell, crashing into the unsuspecting soldiers like a tsunami. Swords clashed and shouts of alarm filled the air as the enemy scrambled to mount a defense. Arrows rained down from the battlements, striking down those who attempted to rally their forces. Out of a side door Romenia burst into the courtyard, a war cry on her lips and a force of Water house guards at her back. They cut through those who opposed them as they made their way to their queen.

Ros was in the thick of it. Her sword clattered to the ground, forgotten as soon as the need for secrecy ended. She cast her power out and sent blasts of water and fire and air hurtling through anyone in her path. When a sword swung her way, she shadow-walked away from the blow, only to find herself in another corner of the courtyard fighting another squad of enemy soldiers. She fought with a single-minded determination, every blast of elemental magic a reminder of why she was here. The faces of her loved ones flashed before her eyes—her parents, Alaric, Cassian, and, most painfully, Elsabet. She prayed her sister was safe, that she wasn't among the traitors they now fought.

Alaric and Cassian fought back-to-back, their movements synchronized as they carved a path through the enemy ranks. Though they made an unlikely pair, their skills were comparable, and they complemented one another as they gave their all for one final push.

Cassian moved with the grace of a seasoned warrior, his sword a blur as he struck down soldier after soldier. He knew where to anticipate the blows before they came, and he was able to avoid every swing that came his way even as he guided Alaric through the crush.

Alaric fought with a ferocity that matched Ros's own, his eyes always flicking to wherever she landed, as if to make sure she was safe. He had vowed to protect her, and he meant to keep that vow, no matter the cost.

As the battle raged on, the tide began to turn in the rebels' favor. The surprise attack had thrown the forces into disarray, and the insurgents seized every advantage. They pushed deeper into the courtyard, driving the enemy back toward the keep.

But just as victory seemed within reach, a shout rang out from the far side of the plaza. Ros turned in time to see a group of soldiers emerging from a hidden passage, their weapons drawn. They were reinforcements—more than the rebels had anticipated.

"Fall back!" Ros shouted, but the warning came too late. The soldiers charged, their numbers threatening to overwhelm them.

Panic surged through the ranks as Alaric's fighters found themselves surrounded. Ros's heart pounded in her chest as she fought to keep her footing, the weight of the battle pressing down on her. They were so close, and yet now it seemed they might be overrun.

But then, from the main gate, a horn sounded—a deep, resonant note that cut through the clamor of battle. Ros's head snapped up, and she saw, to her astonishment, that more figures were emerging from the front entrance of the courtyard. Reinforcements, but not for the traitor's army.

Dryden's diversionary force had arrived.

With a renewed battle cry, the rebels surged forward, the arrival of their comrades giving them the strength to press on. The enemy, caught between the two forces, faltered.

Ros fought her way through the thick of the battle, her

focus on the keep. If they could seize the stronghold, they could hold Water house. They just had to push a little farther.

With Alaric and Cassian at her side, she led the charge, breaking through the enemy's final line of defense. The rebels swarmed the castle, forcing the doors open and flooding inside.

The battle was far from over, but the tide had turned. Water house was within their grasp, and the traitors who had taken it would soon be brought to justice.

As Ros fought her way toward the inner chambers, her thoughts turned to Elsabet. She prayed her sister would be there, waiting for her—not as an enemy, but as an ally. The fate of their family, and perhaps the entire kingdom, hung in the balance.

Twelve

⚬⚬⚬

The heavy doors of the keep groaned as they were forced open, revealing a dimly lit hall beyond. The atmosphere was thick with the scent of smoke and blood, the remnants of battle hanging in the air like a shroud. Ros led the way, her hand raised and ready to press her magic toward any who got in her way. Alaric had retrieved her sword and forced it into her grip, insisting she keep hold of it despite the powerful magic at her fingertips. Her heart pounded as she moved deeper into the fortress. Every step was a reminder of the uncertainty that lay ahead —of what she might find when she finally faced her sister.

Behind Ros, the rebels fanned out, securing the entryway and ensuring that no enemy forces could regroup and launch a counterattack. Alaric and Cassian stayed close at her sides, eyes scanning every shadow, every corner, for any sign of danger. Dryden and Romenia moved with similar caution, their expressions grim as they prepared for whatever lay ahead.

As they reached the end of the hall, a figure emerged from the darkness, stepping into the flickering light of the torches. Ros's breath caught in her throat as she recognized Elsabet standing before them. She looked every bit the part of a traitor—dressed in the garb of Earth house's forces, a sword at her hip, and her countenance cold and unreadable..

"Elsabet," Ros whispered, a mix of relief and dread washing over her. She had found her sister, but the sight of her in the enemy's uniform sent a chill down her spine.

Elsabet's eyes met Rosalinde's, and for a moment, neither of them spoke. The silence between them was heavy with unspoken words, with the weight of all that had happened since they last saw each other.

"So, you've come to reclaim Water house," Elsabet said, her voice calm, almost detached. "And here I thought you might have learned to stay away from places that aren't yours."

Rosalinde's heart sank at the coldness in her sister's voice. "Elsabet, what are you doing here? Why are you with them?"

A bitter smile tugged at the corners of Elsabet's lips. "Why wouldn't I be? This is the winning side, Ros. Did you really think you could waltz in here with your ragtag band of rebels and take it all back? You're a fool."

Dryden stepped forward, his hand on his sword, his eyes narrowing at the princess. "Elsabet, stop this. You don't have to do this. Come with us. We can still make things right."

Elsabet's gaze flicked to Dryden, and her expression hardened. "Make things right? How, by following the likes of you and your merry band? By pretending that everything our ancestors did to this kingdom can be forgiven? You're as naïve as she is."

Ros felt a wave of despair wash over her. This was not the sister she remembered, the sister she had loved and trusted. "Elsabet, please," she pleaded, her voice breaking. "We can still fix this and fight together."

For a moment, it seemed as though something flickered in Elsabet's eyes, a hint of the girl Ros had once known. But then, just as quickly, it was gone, replaced by cold resolve.

"You're too late, Ros," Elsabet said, drawing her sword. "You should have stayed away."

Before Ros could react, Elsabet lunged forward, her blade aimed at Ros's heart. Ros lifted the sword Alaric had forced her to keep, though she was too shocked at Elsabet's actions to do more than hold it in front of her. But as the two sisters' blades clashed, Elsabet shifted ever so slightly, just enough to avoid the fatal blow she had been poised to deliver. At the same moment, the sound of heavy footsteps echoed through the hall. Graeme Monsanato, the deceptive Air house mage who had played all of them, emerged from the adjacent hall. He was flanked by a group of soldiers, their faces twisted with malevolent glee.

"Well, well, what have we here?" Graeme sneered, his

eyes gleaming with malice. "The prodigal daughter returns, only to find that her sister has finally seen the light. It's almost poetic, really. The two of you, locked in battle, just as it should be."

Elsa used her sword to push back and disengage, though her eyes never left Ros. She sidled over to Graeme's side; the elementalist put his arm over Elsabet's shoulders as his terrible smile grew larger.

Ros thought back to Graeme's words from when he'd first taken her to Air house. He had promised that if she wouldn't commit to his plans and do his bidding, she would be eliminated in favor of her sister. Graeme had planned to ally himself with Elsabet, wed her, and have her murdered so that he could take control of the throne. From the looks of it, his plan was well on its way.

Ros gritted her teeth, her mind racing as she struggled to understand what was happening. Had Elsabet not seen through his lies? Elsa had attacked her, had chosen to stand with Graeme. But something in her sister's eyes, in the way she had hesitated for just a moment, gave Ros pause. Was this truly betrayal, or was there something more?

A sudden flurry of motion erupted around them as Graeme's guards pressed forward and attacked the rebels with Ros. She joined the fray, fighting with everything she had, her movements fueled by a desperate need to protect her companions and uncover the truth. She and Elsabet clashed again and again, their swords ringing out in the dimly lit hall.

A leafy vine slashed at Rosalinde's wrist, and she

zapped it with fire to remove it a second later. Elsabet's brows rose as she struck out again with her sword. "Fire? That's new."

"I've learned several new tricks since I last saw you."

"How exciting for you. Too bad it's useless against us."

Elsabet spun away for only a moment, then engaged with a new ferocity. As they locked blades, Elsabet leaned in close, her voice barely above a whisper. "Ros, listen to me. This is all for show."

Ros whirled away from her sister, using the momentum to cast a spray of water at some of the Air house guards. When she moved close to Elsa again, she said, "Hard to believe when you're trying to kill me."

"You know me," she growled.

But did she? The sisters had spent their lives as rivals, not friends. They loved one another, and supported each other as best as they could within their relationship, but it had never been an easy thing between them. Ros knew her sister was clever and resourceful, someone who could think on her feet and adapt. Elsa was far-sighted with her political machinations and intrigue—far more than Ros could ever think of being—so maybe this was all part of some elaborate plan that Ros wasn't privy to.

"I do," Ros said, suddenly much more certain of who her sister was than she'd ever been.

"Then trust me."

Her veins thrummed throughout her body, tingling, as she struggled to process her sister's words and make sense of what was happening. Finally making a decision, Ros gave the tiniest nod of confirmation. She would trust Elsa, for good or ill. She narrowed her eyes at her sister, forcing herself to keep up the pretense that all love was lost between them and pushing Elsabet back as if they were truly enemies.

The battle raged on around them, but Rosalinde's focus was entirely on Elsabet. They continued to exchange blows, but now, Ros noticed something she hadn't before —Elsabet was holding back. She had spent far more time training than Ros had and knew how to use a blade in conjunction with her magic. She could have disarmed Ros at any moment; instead, her precise strikes lacked the deadly intent that Ros had first feared and served to make it appear that Ros was more skilled than she actually was.

Finally, with a sudden maneuver, Elsabet stripped Ros of her weapon, causing her sword to clang onto the floor. Elsa somehow made it look like a spectacular victory against an equally skilled opponent rather than the easy win that it was. Elsabet stepped forward, her blade poised to deliver the final blow against her sister—but instead, she flipped her sword so that Ros could grab the hilt and urgently said, "Go for Graeme. Now."

Ros didn't hesitate. Trusting Elsa with all her heart, she spun on her heel and charged at Graeme, who had been caught off guard by the sudden change in the fight. With a powerful thrust, Ros drove Elsa's sword into Graeme's chest, the traitor's eyes widening in shock before he crumpled to the ground. The room fell silent as the Air house mage's lifeless body hit the floor.

The rebels dispatched the traitors with ease after that. With their leader dead, most of them surrendered immediately, though a few fought until their very last breath. Ros ignored all the things happening around her as she stood panting, her sword dripping with blood, her mind reeling from what had just happened. She looked up at Elsabet, her heart pounding with a mix of fear and hope.

"Elsabet...?" she said, her voice trembling.

Elsabet's cold facade finally broke. She said, "I'm sorry, Ros. I had to make them believe I was on their side. It was the only way I could get close enough to bring them down."

Tears welled in Ros's eyes as she realized the truth. Elsabet had never been a traitor. She had been playing a dangerous game, risking everything to protect her family and their kingdom from within.

Ros rushed forward, pulling her sister into a tight embrace. "He told me he'd been working on winning you to his side, that he'd plotted to make you queen, marry you, and murder you. I thought I'd lost you to his plans," she whispered, her voice choked with emotion.

Elsabet held her tightly, her own tears falling freely now. "You never lost me. I was always with you, even if it didn't seem like it."

"It seemed like everything he'd wanted was coming true."

"It's a fool who tells his ploys to his enemy," Elsa said. She pulled back from Ros and brushed back a loose strand of her sister's strawberry blonde hair. "I knew his plans before he did. You should've known I'd be smarter than to let him get his way."

After taking a moment to truly realize what had happened, Ros leaned close to Elsa's ear and said, "Father is safe and well. What of Mother?"

Elsa sighed. "She's... contained."

"Contained?" Ros repeated.

"It's a long story, and not one for prying ears. But don't worry—we can figure it out together."

As the rest of the rebels gathered around them, the weight of the battle lifted from their shoulders. The traitors were defeated, and Water house was theirs once more. But more importantly, Ros had found her sister again, not as an enemy, but as an ally. Whatever else came would face the might of the Managold sisters. They would rebuild what had been broken and forge a new future for their kingdom —one where betrayal and deceit would no longer hold sway, and where the bonds of family would be stronger than ever before.

Thirteen

The dawn broke over Water house, its golden light casting long shadows across the bloodstained courtyard. The fortress was theirs, but the cost of victory was evident in the weary faces of the rebels and the bodies of the fallen. Ros stood at the top of the battlements, gazing out over the land, her thoughts a storm of conflicting emotions. Beside her, Elsabet was silent, the weight of recent revelations hanging heavily between them.

Alaric, Cassian, Dryden, Brisa, and Kaith joined them, their expressions grim as they surveyed the aftermath of the battle. There was a sense of relief, but it was tempered by the knowledge that their true fight was far from over.

"Graeme is dead, and Gaius—elements help him—has been taken by the Orb of Nullus. I don't know if there is a return from the orb, or if he is gone forever, but for now he is no longer a concern," Cassian began, his voice low and steady. "But there are still shadows in the land. The darkness remains. We're on the brink of a class war, and the things that have led us here won't be so easily defeated."

Ros nodded, her mind racing as she considered their options. Their kingdom had changed drastically over the course of the last two months, or at least now the truth of what Talabrih truly was had become apparent. She wanted to make the world that came out of this turmoil better for all of her people, but she wasn't sure where to start.

"We need allies," Ros said, her voice firm. "More than just the rebels, though they have been instrumental in what we've done. If we're going to stop Talabrih from falling completely apart, we need to band together and find a way through this for everyone. There are still other houses—other leaders—who will stand with us if given the chance."

Alaric crossed his arms, his brow furrowed in thought. "And plenty who will resist. What you're talking about is a complete overhaul of the systems they've held in place for their entire lives, and the lives of their ancestors. Just because we want something better doesn't mean they will all be willing to join us."

"It's true," Cassian said. "Though not everyone fell to the darkness that Gaius and Graeme brought into our kingdom, that doesn't make them allies. There are those who cling to the outdated ways with every fiber of their being and will not change, especially not for a young, inexperienced queen."

"We can bring my father back," Ros said.

"No," Alaric and Cassian said at the same time.

Ros smiled faintly at their unexpected agreement,

despite not fully understanding their objection. "The old leaders would rally to my father, especially knowing we have a real chance of winning."

"What sort of victory will we have if your father is in charge?" Alaric asked. "He has been on the throne for the last two decades and done nothing to help his people. Not unless they were noble mages."

"We need a representative for everyone," Cassian said.

Ros tilted her head at his words, an idea forming. "A council."

"What use is the house council?" Dryden asked.

"That's not what she means," Elsa said. "My brilliant sister is suggesting a group of representatives that is inclusive of everyone, not just the house rulers."

Ros said, "It would provide us with the opportunity to hear what each group needs and serve as a starting point to make changes. Maybe we can avoid things becoming more violent if we establish that we're trying to be better."

"They'll be hesitant—all of them," Kaith said, her tone cautious. "Even if it could work eventually, it might not be enough right now. People are angry, and this fight has been brewing for a long time. And the current leaders will never go for something that could limit their power."

Alaric said, "We need to show the people that we have the strength to lead this struggle, and make sure the house rulers know that we're not just another group of rebels waiting to be crushed."

"We have the queen," Brisa said, smiling as she nodded to Ros. "It's hard to argue with that."

"We have three queens," Cassian said, looking from Ros, to Elsabet, to Brisa. "The one who was named, the one who took her place in Gaius and Graeme's coup, and the one who would rather remain in the shadows."

"There is only one queen. I denounce any claims to the throne and pledge fealty to my sister, Queen Rosalinde Adara Managold," Elsabet said.

"You have no aspirations to be queen?" Dryden asked.

Elsa shook her head. "I never have. They needed someone to be a placeholder for their plans, someone who the nobles would accept, and someone they thought they could manipulate."

Ros laughed. "They chose poorly."

Elsa smiled at her sister. "If only they'd been privy to every time mother has referred to me as 'willful.' They certainly would have chosen someone else."

"Willful, stubborn, proud, and too clever for your own good," Ros said.

"Yes, those are my best qualities."

"And you?" Dryden said, nodding to Brisa.

"I'm unsure why I'm even part of this conversation."

"Probably because you're the Delos Santos heir," Alaric said with a shrug. She glared at him, and he rolled his eyes. "Come on, Bri, everyone here knows. What we don't know is why you want to deny your name, your birthright."

"I have no desire for power. I've seen what it does to people, how it controls and binds them without them ever realizing it is simply another cage. Freedom to do as I wish is far too valuable for me to give up."

"So, you won't take all the power and riches and prestige that come along with the throne?" Dryden asked.

"There's no need for those things in my life."

"What do you need?" Elsabet asked.

Brisa met her eyes, lips turning up ever so slightly. "A full belly, a warm place to lay my head, and a willful, stubborn, proud, too clever woman at my side."

Elsabet's eyes went wide at Brisa's words and she didn't seem to have a response. Cassian, a wide grin on his face, squeezed Brisa's shoulder as he said, "Well then, I guess we're settled at one queen with many friends."

"That seems like a positive spin if anyone tries to challenge her rule," Dryden said. "Especially as Fire house considers itself a friend to our queen."

"It helps, but doesn't fix everything. Traditionalists could easily claim we're forcing Rosalinde to make changes, convince themselves that a coup is their only way to save her from us," Kaith said.

"It's happened before," Cassian said. All eyes turned to him, and he said, "Haven't you heard of the Rancel rebellion?"

"They're house-born, Cas," Brisa said in way of explanation.

Cassian smirked at her as if there was a joke between them, but didn't elaborate on it. He looked to Rosalinde and said, "About sixty years ago there was an uprising of magicless. They were led by a lower nobleman from Fire house, Drewan Rancel, a distant kin of the le Fevre family. He recognized the troubles of the magicless and decided to do something about it. Made it further than anyone expected until a group of mages decided they needed to save Rancel from those who they claimed had taken him hostage. His rebellion ended with all of his co-conspirators dead, and him recanting on everything he'd been trying to do."

The words sat thick between them. After a moment, Rosalinde said, "No matter what happens, I will not turn my back on the people of Talabrih. If that means my life is forfeit alongside theirs, so be it."

Alaric stared at her, pride, admiration, and pain swirling through his gaze. "We won't let it come to that."

"You can't know that," Ros said.

"I will do everything in my power—"

"Alaric," she said, putting her hand on his arm, "you may not be able to stop it. I appreciate your dedication to me and to the cause, but I don't want you to jeopardize yourself or your people on my behalf. You've already done enough in helping take Water house back."

"Now we must rely on a more delicate touch to push things in our favor," Elsabet said.

"That's not exactly in the wheelhouse of this group," Cassian said, a smile curling up one side of his mouth.

"Speak for yourself," Brisa said. "I am nothing if not delicate."

Stifling a laugh, Elsabet said, "All I'm saying is that we need to consider new allies, especially those with a silver tongue who might lean our way."

Alaric huffed, and said, "I may not be the ally you

want, but I'm the one you've got. I'll leave it up to you to figure out how to use me best. We've come this far together. There's no turning back now. And if that means you send me headlong into the unknown armed with only my wits, I'll go where you wish."

Kaith grinned, humor clear in her eyes. "Well, it wouldn't be an adventure if it didn't involve a little bit of suicidal bravery, would it? And trusting in your wits alone would be just that."

Alaric cast her a glare for the jab, but returned her smile when he noticed the manner in which she was looking at him. Ros caught the interaction between them too, and couldn't help but notice how the Fire house spy gazed at him like he hung the moon. She had spoken of him being handsome, and the way she stared at him now made it clear that she thought highly of him for more than just his good looks.

Ros allowed herself a small smile at that. She wondered if Alaric had noticed that the spy admired him, or if his love for the rebellion kept him distracted from the possibilities of what could be. Once, she would have been a jealous mess from seeing someone look at Alaric like that; now though, all she wanted for him was happiness wherever he could find it.

As the group discussed their next steps, Dryden pulled Ros aside, his expression troubled. "There's something else you should know, Ros," he breathed. "Word of what happened here will spread quickly, and Air house won't take it lightly. The Lord Ruler of Air house, Hessian

Barclay, might claim he had nothing to do with Graeme's plans, but I firmly doubt the truth in that. He's going to retaliate, and though it might be quiet and delayed to avoid suspicion, he'll target our weaknesses when he does—our people, our homes, anything we leave unguarded. We need to be prepared for that."

Ros met her friend's gaze, the weight of his words settling heavily on her. "I know," she whispered. "But we can't afford to be defensive. We have to strike first, before he has an opportunity to regroup and make new plans. His hands are all over this—he's been undermining my family and vying for the throne for years—and we can't give him a chance to try something new."

Dryden nodded, though there was still a shadow of worry in his eyes. "Just be careful, Ros. Barclay is danger-ous. He may not possess the same evil that Gaius had, or the same cunning that Graeme had, but that doesn't make him less threatening than the other enemies we've faced. He's treacherous, with a deceptively refined facade covering a vicious blade ready to gut you. With his other plans disrupted, he'll be desperate. Don't underestimate him."

Ros nodded, taking in Dryden's warning. He was right, she knew, but there was no route to proceed without inter-acting with the Air house lord. She just had to figure out how to manipulate him to her cause before he could enact new plans to disrupt what she needed to do.

As the sun continued to rise, the group dispersed to make preparations for the coming journey. They would need to travel far and wide to gather the allies they needed, to strengthen their forces before all of Talabrih erupted into civil war. The road ahead would be long and perilous, but they had no choice. The stakes had never been higher, and the fate of the kingdom rested on their shoulders. But with Elsabet at her side, with Dryden, Cassian, Brisa, Alaric, and Kaith ready to fight with her, Ros felt a surge of hope.

Together, they could face what was to come. And they would win.

Fourteen

The halls of Water House were eerily quiet as Ros and Elsabet made their way toward their mother's chambers. The recent battle had left a heavy atmosphere, and though they had reclaimed their ancestral home, a sense of unease lingered in the air.

Ros glanced at her sister, whose face was set in a determined mask. Elsabet's jaw was clenched, and her hands were curled into fists at her sides. The tension between them had eased since discovering Elsabet was on her side, despite initially seeming to be aligned with their enemies. But now, as they approached their mother's door, that tension had returned and become even more pronounced. Ros wasn't sure if it was because of the animosity that always seemed to rouse at the queen's presence, or if Elsabet was simply too nervous about Sariyah's situation to allow any vulnerability, even where her sister was concerned.

"Are you ready for this?" Ros asked quietly, stopping just outside the ornate wooden door.

Elsabet's eyes flickered with uncertainty for a moment before she nodded. "We need to know where she stands, Ros. If she's truly sided with Gaius—"

Ros didn't let her finish the thought. "We'll find out soon enough."

She pushed open the door, and together they stepped into the dimly lit chamber. Ros felt the ward as they passed through, the suppression of magic that kept her mother contained in this room. Sariyah was standing by the window, her back to them, staring out at the gardens below. The room was stark, without decoration or the flora Ros normally saw wherever her mother was. It was also unusually cold, a direct contrast to the warmth Ros remembered radiating from her mother's magic. Their mother's presence had always brought comfort and security, a feeling of wholeness like Ros normally felt in nature. Though the queen had sometimes been distant, and had never been particularly open to her daughters, she had never seemed outright hostile either.

Until now. As Ros looked at her now, she felt a chill run down her spine.

"Mother," Ros called softly.

Sariyah didn't turn immediately, but after a moment, she slowly pivoted to face them. Her expression was unreadable, her eyes devoid of the affection they had once known. Instead, there was a calculating gleam in her gaze, as if she were assessing them like one might size up an opponent. Their mother had always been the parent who pitted them against one another, who pushed them to be more in whatever they were doing, the one with ambition; still, she had never been so cold, so absolutely empty of any shred of feeling for them.

"Rosalinde. Elsabet," Sariyah said, her voice calm and even. "You've come back."

Ros took a hesitant step forward, searching her mother's face for any sign of the woman she had known. "We have, Mother. Water House is ours again. We fought hard, but we—"

"I know," Sariyah interrupted, her tone icy. "You've reclaimed the keep, contained Gaius, destroyed Graeme, and you've secured the loyalty of Fire and Night house. I suppose you'll be looking for new allies now to strengthen your power."

Ros and Elsabet exchanged a quick, startled glance. They had told no one about Gaius being contained except for their small group of friends, and they had only just discussed the Fire house loyalty after Cassian shadow-walked Dryden home to speak with his cousin.

"How do you know that?" Elsabet asked, her voice laced with suspicion.

Sariyah's lips curved into a faint smile, but it didn't reach her eyes. "Do you think you're the only one with eyes in the castle, little dove? You want to be a master of spies, but didn't think to check who else your informants might report to?"

"Are you saying—"

"I'm saying I have my ways."

"That's not an answer, Mother," Ros pressed, her unease growing.

"It's the best you'll receive from me."

"You've always been able to sense things, to understand the tides before they change," Ros said. "But this feels different. What's going on?"

Sariyah's smile faded, and she turned back to the window, her hands clasped behind her back. "There are many things in this world you do not understand, Rosalinde. Forces at play that you are only beginning to grasp."

Rosalinde's heart sank at her mother's words. There was a coldness in Sariyah's voice that was so unlike her, so distant. "What are you saying?"

"I'm saying that this war is far from over," Sariyah replied, her gaze fixed on the horizon. "And the choices you make now will determine whether you survive it."

Elsabet took a step closer, her voice tight with emotion. "What has happened to you? You're not the woman we knew. You sound like... like him."

Sariyah turned to face them again, her expression hardening. "Like who, Elsabet?"

"Gaius," she whispered.

"You think he's corrupted me? Twisted me into some kind of puppet?"

Elsabet flinched at the sharpness in Sariyah's tone, but she didn't back down. "You're not yourself. The mother who raised us would never speak like this, never align herself with a monster like him."

"People change," Sariyah said coldly. "Circumstances force them to adapt, to make tough decisions."

Ros's mind raced, trying to piece together the puzzle before her. "What are you saying? Are you working with Gaius on purpose, or is he making you?"

Sariyah's eyes flicked to Ros, a flash of something—regret?—crossing her features before her expression hardened again. "The world is not as black and white as you'd like to believe."

"So, a mixture of the two? We can work with that and find a way to help you."

"I'm doing what I must to ensure our survival," Sariyah said. "There's nothing for you to do but stay out of the way, and you're doing a terrible job of that."

Ros felt a surge of anger and fear rise within her. "Survival? At what cost? How many lives are you willing to sacrifice?"

Sariyah's gaze sharpened, and for a moment, Ros thought she saw a flicker of the mother she remembered, the woman who had always protected them. But it was gone as quickly as it had appeared. "As many as it takes! I am protecting you. Everything I have done has been done for you."

Elsabet shook her head, tears welling in her eyes. "This isn't protection, it's betrayal."

Sariyah's expression remained stony, unmoved by Elsabet's words. "You're young. You don't understand what is

THE FLAME OF FIRE HOUSE

required to survive in this world, to protect the ones you love. Sometimes, you have to make alliances you never wanted. Sometimes, you have to do things that others will never understand."

Ros felt a chill settle in her chest as she looked at the woman before her, a woman who was so different from the mother she had known. "You're siding with him," she mumbled, the realization sinking in. "You've made your choice."

Sariyah's eyes flashed with a mixture of emotions—anger, regret, sadness—but when she spoke, her voice was cold and resolute. "I've made the only choice I could, Rosalinde. I suggest you do the same."

Ros opened her mouth to speak, to argue, but the words caught in her throat. What could she say? How could she reach her mother when it seemed she had already made up her mind?

"Please, Mother," Elsabet said, taking a step closer. "Come back with us. We can protect you, we can—"

"Protect me?" Sariyah cut her off, her voice edged with something sharp, almost mocking. "You think you can protect me from what's coming? From the forces that are already in motion?"

Elsabet recoiled as if struck, and Ros felt her heart twist at the sight of her sister's pain. Though Ros and her mother had never been close, Elsabet and Sariyah had been thick as thieves through the years. As much as Ros was like her father, Elsabet had always seemed like a direct copy of the queen. Seeing her dismiss Elsabet so easily, and the pain it caused her younger sister, was hard to watch.

"This conversation is over," Sariyah said, turning her back to them once more. "You've made your choices, and I've made mine. I suggest you leave before it's too late."

Ros stared at her mother's back, feeling a mix of anger, sorrow, and helplessness wash over her. She wanted to scream, to shake Sariyah out of whatever trance she was in, but she knew it would do no good. Whatever had changed in their mother, it was deep, and it was dark.

"Come on, Elsabet," Ros said quietly, gently taking her sister's arm. "Let's go."

Elsabet hesitated, her eyes locked on Sariyah, but finally she nodded, allowing Ros to guide her out of the room. As they stepped back into the hallway, Ros closed the door behind them, shutting out the cold, distant figure that had once been their mother.

For a moment, neither of them spoke. The silence between them was heavy, filled with unspoken fears and shattered hopes.

Elsabet's voice was a fragile whisper as she asked, "What are we going to do?"

Ros didn't have an answer. She didn't know how to fight this, how to bring back the mother they had lost. All she knew was that they couldn't give up, no matter how impossible the situation seemed.

"We'll figure it out," Ros said, her voice trembling slightly. "We have to."

But as they walked away, leaving their mother's chambers behind, Ros couldn't shake the feeling that something vital had been lost—something they might never get back.

THE CHILL of the early morning clung to Ros's skin as she stood on the balcony of the newly reclaimed Water House. Below, the courtyard was littered with the remnants of the battle—broken weapons, discarded shields, and the bodies of the fallen, both ally and enemy alike. She had insisted on seeing the aftermath herself, not because she wanted to revel in their victory, but because she needed to remember the cost. Each life lost was a reminder of the heavy burden she bore as the leader of this fractured kingdom.

The wind picked up, carrying with it the scent of blood and smoke. Ros tightened her cloak around her shoulders, trying to shake off the creeping sense of dread that had settled deep in her bones. Water House was hers again, but at what price? The losses were heavy, and the faces of the dead haunted her every time she closed her eyes.

Her thoughts were interrupted by the sound of footsteps approaching. She turned to see Cassian stepping onto the balcony, his expression as weary as her own. His dark eyes met hers, consuming all the light around them and rendering their world in muted grays. For a moment, they simply stood there in silence, the weight of the recent events pressing down on them.

"How are you holding up?" he asked, his voice soft.

Ros forced a small smile. "I've been better. But we've won, at least for now."

Cassian nodded, though there was no triumph in his expression. "The others are gathering in the great hall. Alaric wants to discuss our next move."

Ros sighed, turning back to the courtyard. "There's always a next move, isn't there? No time to rest, to grieve."

"We don't have the luxury of rest," Cassian said, stepping closer to her and pressing his palm on her back where he rubbed small, steady circles of comfort. "Not while the kingdom is still at war."

Ros knew he was right, but the thought of continuing this fight, of losing more people, weighed heavily on her. "I saw my mother," she said, her voice barely above a whisper. "She was with them, Cassian. She's chosen their side."

Cassian's expression darkened, and he placed a comforting hand on her shoulder. "We don't know that for sure, Ros. The magic Gaius wielded may still be holding her, or she might have been coerced, or—"

"She wasn't coerced," Ros interrupted, her voice tinged with bitterness. "She was so... cold, so distant. I barely recognized her. Whatever loyalty she had to me, to our family, it's gone."

Cassian didn't respond immediately, his brow furrowed in thought. "Maybe it's not gone. Perhaps it's buried deep down, under layers of fear and anger. But that doesn't mean it can't be brought back."

Ros wanted to believe him, but the image of her mother's icy gaze was burned into her memory. "I'm not sure I can reach her. Not anymore."

Cassian squeezed her shoulder gently. "You're stronger than you think. Stronger than any of us. If anyone can bring her back, it's you."

Ros gave a small nod, though she wasn't entirely convinced. "I hope you're right."

After a moment, Cassian said, "We should go. The others are waiting."

Ros hesitated, her gaze lingering on the courtyard one last time. "Do you think we're doing the right thing? All this fighting, all this death... is it worth it?"

Cassian's eyes softened as he looked at her. "It has to be, Ros. Because if it isn't, then everything we've done, everything we've lost, would all be for nothing."

Ros let out a shaky breath, nodding as she turned to follow Cassian back inside. As they walked through the dimly lit corridors of Water House, the weight of their responsibility settled heavily on her shoulders. She could hear the murmur of voices growing louder as they approached the great hall, where Alaric and the others were waiting.

When they entered the room, the conversation ceased, and all eyes turned to Ros. Alaric was standing at the head of the table, a map of Talabrih spread out before him. Dryden, Florian, and several other key allies were gathered around, their expressions grim and focused.

"Ros," Alaric greeted her with a nod. "We were just

discussing our next steps. We need to hurry if we're going to capitalize on this victory."

Ros stepped forward, her gaze sweeping over the faces of those gathered. "What's the plan?"

"We've secured Water House, but Graeme's army is still a force to be reckoned with," Alaric began. "With Gaius contained, their leadership is fractured, but that won't last long. We need to press our advantage before they can regroup."

Florian leaned forward, his expression intense. "We've received reports that Graeme's remaining forces are gathering in the forests outside of Earth House. If we strike now, we can catch them off guard and potentially end this war before it escalates further."

Ros considered his words, her mind racing with the implications. Her mother was from Earth House. Was the entire force of Earth elementalists entangled in this mess with Air house? Had they sold their allegiance to Hessian Barclay, or was there a misunderstanding or failure in their information? The forces weren't gathering *in* Earth house, which seemed like a good sign. The Lady Ruler, Valeria Auguste, was a bold, brave woman who seemed unlikely to allow another house to gather their forces in her domain. Hopefully, there was more to her than just protecting her space.

Still, trusting Valeria to do what was best for Talabrih was a dangerous gamble. She held house loyalty above all else, and Ros couldn't be certain she wouldn't fight on Air house's side for the promise of something that would help her house. She needed more information, but how could she get it without risking one of her people or trusting the words of someone with their own agenda?

"What about the people?" Ros asked, her voice steady despite the turmoil in her heart. "The civilians caught in the crossfire? We've already lost so many. I don't want more innocent lives on my conscience."

Dryden, who had been silent until now, spoke up. "We'll do everything we can to protect them, Ros, but we can't afford to wait. The longer we delay, the more time our enemies have to regroup and strengthen their defenses."

Ros looked at Cassian, searching for his input. He met her gaze, his expression thoughtful. "I agree with Dryden. We're stretched thin, and it's a risk, but it's one we have to take. If we can end this now, it's worth it."

Ros knew they were right. Despite her reservations, she couldn't ignore the urgency of the situation. They had come too far to back down now. But even as she nodded in agreement, a part of her couldn't shake the feeling that there was something they were missing, some threat lurking in the shadows, waiting to strike.

"Then it's decided," Ros said, her voice firm. "We'll move on Earth House. But we do it carefully, and we do it with the protection of our people as our top priority."

Alaric gave a nod of approval, a rare smile tugging at the corners of his mouth. "We'll start preparations immediately. I'll organize the troops and have them ready to march by nightfall. We'll need to move quickly if we're going to surprise them, but I don't want to risk tiring them out. It's already been a helluva few days."

"We can shadow-walk them," Cassian said. "A few at a time, at least."

"And risk exhausting you before the battle?" Brisa asked, concern in her tone.

"Let's start with scouts to get the best information for us. Ros and I can both use the power, so we'll split the chore of getting them there after we get a plan in place."

As the others discussed the logistics of the assault, Ros's mind drifted back to Queen Sariyah. She couldn't shake the image of her mother's cold, accusing eyes. What had happened to the woman she once knew? Was she truly lost to her now, or was there still a chance to bring her back?

The questions lingered in Rosalinde's mind as she listened to the discussions around her. The fate of the kingdom rested on their shoulders, but so too did the fate of her family. And no matter what happened next, Ros was determined to see both through to the end.

Fifteen

The moon hung low in the sky, casting a pale glow over the dense forest surrounding Water House. Ros stood at the window, her eyes scanning the grounds as the cool night wind whipped past her. The sounds of murmured conversations and the occasional clink of armor filled the air behind her, but her thoughts were elsewhere. She and Cassian had gathered their scouts who would shadow-walk to Earth house in a secluded chamber of Water House. The room, usually a place of strategic planning, was now alive with the quiet urgency of impending action. Maps and charts adorned the walls, each one marked with the intricate details of their kingdom's key locations.

"We're almost ready," Cassian said as he appeared by her side, his dark eyes catching the faint light.

Ros gave a tight nod, her mind heavy with the weight of their upcoming assault on the Air House forces. Every step they took brought them closer to victory—or to another devastating loss. She couldn't afford any more mistakes.

Cassian moved closer, his hand brushing hers. "You don't have to carry this all on your own."

"I know," she whispered, though the burden still felt like hers to bear. "But this has to work. We don't have the numbers for a drawn-out battle. A quick, coordinated strike is the only way."

He gave a small, confident smile. "That's why we're shadow-walking the scouts. We'll know every weak point in their defenses before dawn."

She sent him to review the final details of their mission with the team. The dozen scouts nodded along, taking in every word. He paused and turned to her so that she could speak to her people before they left.

Ros moved to the center of the room, her presence commanding yet weary. She had rested for a few hours, bathed, and dressed in the colors of her house. Her cloak, a heavy, fur-lined thing that was a blue so deep it was bordering on black, draped elegantly over her shoulders. She'd asked for pants and a tunic, despite the optics of it and her sister's desire for her to parade around the castle in her finest gowns. Elsabet herself preferred pants over dresses, boots over heels, but she wanted Ros to present herself as a traditional ruler who just so happened to have won her throne back from traitors and immediately returned to the ways everyone was comfortable with. Elsa didn't want her to actually go back to the old ways, just give the appearance of them until they could sort out where the nobles stood.

She thought she'd talk to her father about it and see what his opinion was, but when Cassian brought him back from Fire house that morning, he'd gone straight to the healing wing and started working. There would be time to get his advice and sort out what she should do later; for now, she was comfortably dressed and fully ready to shadow-walk their people across the land.

"Remember," Ros began, her voice steady, "our aim is to gather intelligence on the Air House forces. We need to know their numbers, their positions, and any weaknesses we can exploit. Stealth is our greatest ally."

Cassian nodded, his black eyes meeting hers. "They're ready. They can move unseen, but we must remain vigilant. Any mistake could cost us dearly."

Ros nodded to the two in the back. "You will go into Earth house. We need to know what's going on, how much of what Air house is doing aligns with our friends at Earth. If you think you're in danger—any of you—get out. I will not have you sacrificing yourself for this."

One by one, Ros met the scouts' eyes and made sure they each understood their importance to her, that no life was worth losing for the information they were gathering. With a final nod, Ros signaled the commencement of the mission. The scouts dispersed into two groups of six, all prepared to walk through the shadows.

Cas stepped close to Ros and murmured, "Are you sure you can handle this many at once?"

"I've done it before."

"Not with six other people. It will drain you a lot faster. I just don't want you to get stranded at Earth house. Or worse..."

"Worse?"

A shadow flitted across Cassian's face, gone before Ros could parse it. He shook his head and said, "Just be careful."

Cassian and Ros each took the hands of a group of them and stepped through the shadows to the location they'd agreed upon. The world around them darkened, and Ros felt the familiar sensation of her body being pulled across a great distance, as if they were passing through the void itself. This time, however, she was in charge. She watched the colors pass by out of the corners of her eyes, but kept her focus on the path ahead of her. She had to concentrate on her feet and every step they made if she was going to get the scouts through safely.

It was harder than the last time Ros shadow-walked. Not fully exhausting, as she'd worried after Cassian's words, but not an effortless task either. It probably didn't help that they were operating on such little sleep. Not to mention that Ros still had yet to eat. She couldn't. Everything the cooks made smelled like the burned flesh, the blood, the scent of death still lingering in the Water house courtyard.

When her feet touched solid ground again, she opened her eyes to see a forested ridge overlooking Earth House. It was quiet—eerily so—beneath them. In the distance, Ros could make out the dark shapes of Air House's forces.

"They're not expecting us to come from this side," Kaith said. "The bulk of their troops are guarding the main road."

Cassian nodded, his eyes scanning the horizon. "Good. We'll set up here. Move fast, stay hidden. We can't afford to give them any warning."

Kaith said, "Back here in three hours, my queen?"

"Yes," Ros said. "Until then, be careful."

After leaving the groups in the forest near Earth house, Ros and Cas returned to their posts at Water house. Since they weren't scheduled to check in with the scouts for three hours, they had a bit of time to fill. Until then, there was plenty to do to prepare the rest of the forces.

Hours passed in tense anticipation. When the three-hour mark neared, Ros returned to pace the ready room, her mind racing with possibilities and contingencies. The sound of footsteps echoed softly as Cassian approached her. He looked around the room and asked, "Where is everyone?"

Ros shrugged. "Sleeping? Worrying? I don't know."

"We've received the initial report," he said, his expression thoughtful. "Do you want to call them in?"

"No. We'll fill them in later. Let them have peace for a few hours."

"What about you?"

She gave him a sad smile. "Peace isn't on my horizon, even though it is all I want."

Cas put a hand on her shoulder. "Keep wanting it and eventually we'll get there."

Ros nodded. "Enough of that. Tell me what happened with the scouts."

He had attended the meetup himself, where Kaith was set to make her first report. Cas had made Rosalinde promise to remain at Water house in case something had gone wrong. Fortunately, it seemed that everything was going better than they could have anticipated. He held out a hastily drawn but detailed layout of the Air House defenses, including troop placements and fortifications.

"Their forces are concentrated in the eastern quadrant. Heavy archers at the walls and infantry near the gate. They're not letting anyone in or out."

Ros examined the map, her strategic mind already piecing together their next moves. "You think Earth house is under siege then?"

He shook his head. "That might have been the plan, but Earth house is getting through their lines."

"There's a secondary supply route through the old aqueducts, which is probably unguarded. Not many know about it. Valeria's troops might not be able to shadow-walk, but I guarantee they can move in and out of Earth house if they need to."

Cassian frowned, pointing to a section of the map. "Could we use that to get in?"

Before Ros could respond, the door to the chamber creaked open. She turned to see Romenia in the doorway. The normally composed woman wore a crease between her brows, and though it wasn't much, it was like a beacon on the neutral face Romenia always had.

"Enter," Ros said. "Romenia, please, tell me what's wrong."

The guard stepped inside, her expression grim. "There's someone here to see you."

"That doesn't explain what has you so concerned."

Her brown eyes found Rosalinde's periwinkle gaze. "It's Lord Cavoll of Air house."

Ros's brow furrowed in confusion. "Father or son?"

"Son. He says it's urgent," Romenia replied, her tone indicating the seriousness of the matter. "He's requested a private audience."

Ros nodded, already on edge. Brensen Cavoll and his family had been an ally of Water house in the past, but their involvement had been limited, preferring to stay out of the internal conflicts that had been tearing Talabrih apart. They had been more prominent in court when Ros was younger and first manifested her powers. Brensen was a Stormcalmer and had been instrumental in Rosalinde's training—or at least in preventing everyone else from being injured during her training. For them to get involved now meant something significant was happening.

"Bring him in," Ros said as she stood, straightening her clothes and preparing herself for whatever news was about to come.

Romenia gave a curt nod and left the room. A moment later, she returned with Lord Cavoll—a tall, imposing man with sharp features and storm-gray eyes that held an intensity that matched the urgency of his arrival. He bowed deeply to Ros before straightening, his expression grave.

"Your Majesty," Lord Cavoll began, his voice low and formal. "Thank you for seeing me on such short notice."

"Of course, Lord Cavoll. Brensen? Can I still call you that, old friend?" Ros replied, motioning for him to take a seat at the table in the center of the room.

Lord Cavoll smiled, releasing some of the tension on his face. He looked like a completely different man at that moment, losing ten years from his countenance in the blink of an eye.

"Please, Your Majesty," he said with a slight chuckle.

"And I'm still just Ros," she said. "We've known each other too long to adhere to formalities in private."

"It's an immense relief to hear you speak of our friendship. With all the things happening in Air house..." Brensen trailed off.

Ros said, "You have a friend in Water house, my Lord. Now please, tell me what brings you here so urgently."

Lord Cavoll took a seat, his demeanor still tense but less so than before. "I wish I could say this was merely a social visit, but I'm afraid the situation is far more dire. There have been disturbing developments along our border, near the western reaches of Talabrih."

Ros leaned forward, her attention fully focused. "What developments?"

"Reports have been coming in of strange activities in the Calpatherin Mountains," Cavoll explained. "Villages have been abandoned overnight, with no sign of where the inhabitants have gone. Even more troubling, the ground soldiers we sent to investigate have disappeared as well."

Ros's blood ran cold. The Calpatherin Mountains were known for their harsh terrain and superstitions, but this was different—this was something more sinister. "Have you found any evidence of who—or what—might be responsible?"

Lord Cavoll shook his head, frustration clear in his eyes. "None. We've searched the areas, but there are no signs of struggle, no bodies, nothing. It's as if these people simply vanished. And now, rumors are spreading that something unnatural is at work, something that could threaten all of Talabrih."

Ros exchanged a glance with Cassian, who was equally concerned. "Why are you bringing this to me? Where is your Lord Ruler in all this?" she asked, though she had a sinking feeling she already knew the answer.

Brensen's eyes narrowed at the mention of Hessian Barclay. "Lord Barclay is occupied with other things. Foolish things that go against the interests and opinions of the people in Air house."

Ros nodded, acknowledging that she understood what he could not say aloud. Barclay was poised against her, against Water house, but there were those in Air house who still supported her and the throne. Just because he was against her didn't mean the entire house was lost.

"And the other lords chose you to come to me because we have a friendly past."

Brensen nodded. "It was a consideration, yes. To be

honest, when the council met, we weren't sure what reception any of us might receive after the things that happened with Lord Monsanato. You have to know that we were not consulted in your capture, nor that of your father. When we discovered what he'd done, he was banned from Air house. We haven't seen him since."

Ros and Cassian shared a look but didn't comment. Ros knew that was a tidbit to tuck away and discuss later. For now, it seemed that Air house had not learned of what happened to the recently deceased lord.

"Despite all that has happened, I would not turn away one of my people. Even if there are those in Air house who wish me harm."

"That's good news, because this isn't just an Air house problem," Brensen said, his voice firm. "Whatever is happening in those mountains, it's spreading. We had the first reports two weeks ago, and it has spread to the eastern mountain range already. Air house is completely surrounded by this thing. Our position in the sky seems to have spared us, but the people on land... If we don't act quickly, it could cross the mountain range and engulf us all."

Ros felt the weight of his words settle heavily on her shoulders. This was more than just an internal conflict—it was a potential catastrophe that could destabilize the entire kingdom.

"Is there a route this thing seems to be taking?"

"None that we can determine. Though if I had to place

a wager, I would bet Earth house would be the first casualty once it crosses the mountains."

"Winnolds," Cassian said from his position by the window. "It's the only village between Earth house and the mountains that separate Air house from the rest of Talabrih."

Brensen's eyes widened, and he said, "Damn. I forgot about Winnolds. I'll need to send a scout overhead to see if the village is still intact."

Cassian shook his head. "I can shadow-walk there and back faster than a scout."

"No," Ros said quickly. "If the ground troops haven't returned, you can't risk going in on your own."

"I'll be quick."

"No," she said. It was clear by her tone that she was saying this as his queen, not as his friend, or whatever else they were.

He nodded. "As you wish."

"I'll have someone airborne as soon as I can," Brensen said.

"Where are your scouts right now?" Ros asked.

Brensen hesitated, sighed. "With all due respect, Your Majesty, giving away the location of my spies will not happen, even if we are friendly."

The corner of Rosalinde's lip tilted up as she said, "You can't blame me for trying."

"I cannot. Personally, I'd love nothing more than to eliminate the need for them. All four houses have been at odds for too long. Even allies use scouts and spies to protect us from those we should consider friends, family, even."

Ros nodded. "I agree, and I hope we will be able to make those changes by forging relationships based on honesty and trust, not just a mutual agreement to avoid the dangers all out war could bring."

"Perhaps this crisis on the western border is the first step, then."

"What do you propose?" Ros asked, already formulating strategies in her mind.

"We need to combine our forces," Lord Cavoll replied. "Air house is prepared to send troops to investigate and, if possible, to contain whatever this is, but we'll need your support. We can't do this alone."

Ros nodded slowly, understanding the gravity of the situation. "I'll mobilize a contingent to join your forces. We'll need to act quickly before this spreads any further."

"There's more," Lord Cavoll added, his voice dropping to muted tones. "The last report we received mentioned a name—Gaius."

Ros's heart skipped a beat. Gaius had been contained, but his influence—his reach—could still be spreading. "What did they say?"

"Only that his name was spoken by a survivor of one of the smaller villages before they too vanished," Cavoll said, his expression hardening. "Whatever is happening, it's connected to him."

Ros's mind raced. Gaius's power, even in containment inside the Orb of Nullus, could still be a threat. If he had found a way to manipulate events from afar, then this situation was even more dangerous than she had feared.

"We'll leave at once," Ros said, standing. "This cannot wait. Cassian, gather our best troops. We'll head west and meet with Air house's forces."

Cassian nodded, already moving to carry out her orders. Lord Cavoll rose as well, relief evident in his eyes.

"Thank you, Your Majesty. Ros," Cavoll said, bowing again. "Air house will not forget this. I will not forget."

"Neither will I," Ros replied, her voice steely. "We'll end this together."

As Lord Cavoll exited the room, Ros turned to Cassian, her heart pounding with a mix of fear and determination. They had faced battles, death, and magic, but this—this was something different. Something darker.

"We'll need to be ready for anything," Ros said quietly, her gaze distant as she considered the unknown threat lurking in the mountains. "This could change everything."

Cassian placed a reassuring hand on her shoulder. "Whatever it is, we'll stop it."

Ros nodded, grateful for his presence. But as they began to prepare for their journey west, she couldn't shake the feeling that they were about to face an enemy unlike any they had encountered before—a force that could threaten not just the kingdom of Talabrih, but the entire world.

Sixteen

ess than three hours later, Cas and Ros stood on the ridge overlooking Earth house. Cassian had tried to leave Ros waiting in Water house again, but she wouldn't hear of it. Her nerves were on edge, and she needed to see for herself that the scouts they'd brought to gather information were well.

It was early morning, dawn still an hour away. The sky above them was a deep indigo, not yet starting to lighten toward the horizon, though it wouldn't be long now. All around them, the landscape below was cloaked in a quiet, almost eerie stillness. Earth House itself, surrounded by its high walls of protection, blended seamlessly into the dark surrounding it. Nestled in the center of the city, the formidable inner fortress where the Lord Ruler resided had towering spires that rose like jagged teeth against the dark sky, barely perceptible as a slightly darker shade of black.

"Where is Kaith?" Cassian asked, though it was more to himself than to her.

Ros watched the grounds surrounding Earth house, or the parts she could see, at least. Patches of wild grass and gnarled trees had taken root in the tilled land between the treeline and the walls. When the boundaries were erected, someone had made sure to leave space to see anyone who approached. Ros wondered if the Earth house guards sat atop their walls watching the forces surrounding them even now as she looked down at them all.

There was a tension in the air—a sense of anticipation, as if the land itself was holding its breath, waiting for a coming storm. The silence was profound, broken only by the occasional rustle of leaves or the faint call of a distant bird; it was the kind of silence that felt heavy, as if it was merely the prelude to something much darker.

To their left, a shadow emerged and proceeded toward them. Cassian said, "Finally," relief in his voice.

But the person who met them was not Kaith.

"M'lord," the young man said. He removed his hat and dipped his chin low to Ros. "My queen."

"Where is Kaith?"

"I don't know," he said.

"And Maris, Kaith's second?"

The boy shook his head.

"What do you know?" Cassian growled.

Ros put a hand on Cassian's arm to calm him and turned to the boy. "What is your name?"

"Noah."

"Noah," she repeated. She didn't remember seeing him before. "How old are you?"

"Fifteen."

So young. Too young for this sort of thing. She asked, "You're a scout for Water house?"

Noah shook his head. "No, m'lady."

"Why are you here?"

"I was sent to retrieve you."

Cassian cursed. "Who knew we'd be here?" When Noah blanched and cringed away from him, Cas took a deep breath and asked, "Who sent you, kid?"

Kid, Ros thought. Cassian was only five years older than him—so was Ros, for that matter—but they had already faced more than their twenty years should have ever had to see.

"L-lady Zolto," Noah said.

"Larkin?" Ros asked.

Noah nodded. "She wishes to have a meeting with you."

The words left Rosalinde's ears ringing. Larkin had been her closest friend for years, but she'd been blackmailed into conspiring against Ros and presenting herself in opposition to her rule. Though they'd been able to clear it up, Ros still felt hesitant to reach out to Larkin while there were so many moving pieces to all that was happening. She'd felt much the same about her sister, and things had turned out well. Perhaps a meeting with Larkin would offer the same results.

"We'll meet her," Ros said.

"Rosalinde," Cassian groaned.

She glared at him, and he simply shook his head. Ros knew he worried about her exposing herself to danger too often, but if she had learned anything through all of this, it was that rewards required risks. Still, she took Cassian's hesitance into account, knowing he had far more experience at clandestine meetings.

"Go back to your lady and tell her we'll meet her at dawn at her favorite stables. She'll know which ones I mean."

"She needs to come alone," Cassian said. Noah hesitated, as if gathering the nerve to say something, and Cassian said, "Spit it out."

"She won't come alone, m'lord."

"Then we won't see her," Cassian replied.

Ros eyed the boy for a moment, then asked, "Who will she bring?"

"Her brother, most likely. Lord Zolto was with her when she sent me to find you."

Rosalinde said, "Lord Zolto is welcome, if his sister wishes to bring him. No one else."

Noah nodded and bowed to her once more. "Thank you, m'lady. I'll return to them at once."

When the boy was gone, Cassian turned to her and said, "This isn't good."

"It doesn't have to be bad, either."

"Ros, love, our scouts are missing, and you have agreed to meet the person who knew where to send her own messenger to find us. The same person who knows you better than anyone else."

"And her brother," Ros added.

Cassian scrubbed a hand over his face. "And her brother, a man who is definitely in love with you, and by now surely understands that you chose him as your betrothed because you were being blackmailed."

"We don't know that he's in love with me. He was engaged to Elsa after me. Maybe he's just in love with Talabrih."

"Maybe," Cassian said, though his expression showed that he wasn't even entertaining the thought. "Or maybe he's a twice jilted man with a grudge against the Managold sisters. You ran from Water house in the middle of the night to avoid marrying him—"

"There was more to it than that," Ros cut in.

Cas pursed his lips. "You ran. From him. And maybe also the imminent imprisonment you were facing. Then he was pushed over to your sister, but only as a distraction until Graeme had time to move in and take her as his betrothed. There's no way he isn't a little bitter."

"I have known Lyzandor Zolto for years," Ros said. "And I simply cannot believe he would hold any of that against us. He's too good a man to be angry about things out of our control, especially with everything else going on."

"Care to wager? A copper, maybe?"

Ros blinked at the words. "Are you serious? You want to gamble on whether a nobleman from Earth house will be mad that he's not engaged to the most chaotic ruler in the history of Talabrih?"

Cas smiled. "Yes, I am absolutely serious. Though I think you're giving yourself a little too much credit in the chaos department. You're not even half as wild as the stories of Madrina Delos Santos or Vivienne de Fai."

"My competitors for most chaotic have been dead for hundreds of years."

"Fine, maybe you're the most chaotic of our generation," he conceded. "Let them be a guide for who you become, and you can be a historical wild queen for future women in power."

"That sounds like a brilliant idea," she said, smiling broadly.

"For now, my Lady of Chaos, we have a very foolish meeting to attend." He reached his hand out to take hers and said, "Shall we?"

"Wait," she said. "There's still one thing to do before we go."

"And what's that?"

She reached her own hand forward and said, "Shake on the wager."

With a laugh, Cassian took Rosalinde's hand in his own and they disappeared into the shadows.

LARKIN AND LYZANDOR stepped inside the stables behind the Iron Oak Tavern as dawn broke over the horizon. They both wore dark brown cloaks that covered their faces but threw them back as soon as they were under the protection of darkness.

Ros stood against the back wall, using the shadows to disguise her. Cassian was there somewhere, though even Rosalinde couldn't pick him out from the darkness. Ros stared at the woman who had been her best friend for years; Larkin's presence was both a comfort and a source of tension, while Lyzandor's expression and demeanor gave nothing away. Ros stepped forward from the wall, letting the shadows covering her return to their rest. The siblings turned to her, both looking as if they were happy to see her.

"Ros," Larkin greeted, her smile warm yet guarded. "You remembered my favorite stable."

"Hard to forget after the stories you've told me about this place."

Larkin smirked. "I have had some great times here."

"Please do not continue with this conversation," Zandor said with a grimace.

Ros offered a strained smile, her eyes flickering with uncertainty. "You called this meeting, so tell me, what brings us here?"

Lyzandor stepped forward, his expression earnest. "When I learned of what happened—"

Ros cut him off with a swipe of her hand. "You were innocent in all of it."

"That doesn't make it easier to bear. You were going through so much, and I was surely no help, lost in my own world and ignorant of what was happening all around me.

I will spend my life in your service, endeavoring to show you how sorry I am."

"That is all in the past," Ros said. "I only wish to speak of the present."

Zandor swallowed back whatever pleas were on his tongue. Though Ros hadn't been cruel regarding his words, she had been dismissive, and it seemed he was trying to figure out what else he could say.

Instead, Larkin stepped in. "We wanted to offer our assistance. Our Lady Ruler has been reconsidering her position regarding Air house, and we believe we can help bridge the gap between our forces."

"What exactly is her position?" Ros asked.

"Mostly to stay out of the conflict," Larkin said. "But that became impossible when Earth house was the site of battle only days ago."

"And after that happened your Lady Ruler decided letting Air house camp outside her walls was a good idea?"

"When an army shows up at your door and threatens your people unless you agree to house them, there isn't a choice," Zandor said.

"But then they started taking Earth house residents by force, and they have not returned," Larkin said.

"Yet Lady Auguste has still done nothing against the forces?"

"We don't have an army to combat them," Larkin said. "We have mages, sure, and we could fight them a bit. But our people were not prepared for this, and there are not enough of us to battle the force outside our gates."

"But your people *and* ours..." Zandor said, trailing off.

"I see." Ros studied them carefully, sensing the weight of their words. "Your support could be invaluable, but trust is not easily given, especially considering all our houses have been through. How do we know your intentions align with ours?"

Larkin's gaze softened, but there was an edge of caution in her eyes. "We've seen the way things are unfolding, Ros. Valeria remains a friend, but her grip is weakening the longer Air house is camped outside, and there are factions within her court that are sympathetic to your cause. We can act as your eyes and ears inside Earth House."

Ros felt the pull of their offer, the potential advantage it could bring. Yet, the secrets they seemed to possess unnerved her. She wanted to trust them, more than anything else. Her wish was to return to the place where she could count them as friends. Unfortunately, today was not the day for that to happen. "And what of your loyalty? How can we be certain you're not playing a double game?"

Lyzandor placed his hand over his heart. "Mistakes were made, trust broken, but our bond runs deep. We understand your hesitance, and that we will need to work to earn back what was lost. Larkin and I can do that if it means seeing our kingdom restored to peace."

Ros took a deep breath, weighing their plea against the backdrop of recent betrayals. "Very well. You can join our planning phase, but any sign of deceit, and you'll answer to me."

Larkin nodded, a mixture of relief and determination in her eyes. "Understood. We won't let you down."

"One question," Cassian said, stepping from the shadows.

Lyzandor's jaw clenched at the sudden presence of the Night mage, but his voice came out sickly sweet as he asked, "And what's that?"

"Are you angry?"

Zandor's gaze shot to Cassian's. "Am I angry? Of course I am. My queen's life, her future, was upended and altered irreparably. Various nobles and house leaders plotted against the crown. Larkin was forced to act against her best friend, destroying years of trust and love in the process. My house, my *home*, was attacked and my people suffered from the battle forced upon it. How could I not be angry?"

"What about your life?" Cas said.

"My life is forfeit in service of Queen Rosalinde."

"Come on," Cassian said, his voice conspiratorial as a smile slid onto his face. "You were set to marry the highest power in the land, to become king. And you were in love with the woman, to boot."

"Get to the question," Zandor said, teeth gritted.

"Are you bitter that it was all ripped away?"

He dared a brief glance at Ros, then ducked his head. When he spoke, his voice was tinged with a deep sadness. "Is that what this well of pain is? Bitterness? I wouldn't call it that if I was forced to name it. But maybe that's what it is when the hurt is too much to bear without breaking, when your thoughts can't run far enough away from the torture of what you had, what you lost."

"Do you blame her?" Cassian asked.

"Do you?" Lyzandor asked. "She didn't pick you, either. And we both know you thought she would."

Ros was shocked when Cassian said, "Yes, I blame her. I can't shake the fact that Ros didn't trust that we could sort it out together."

Zandor nodded. "She should have told me, given me a chance to prove I was the man she's known all these years instead of the one these lies created."

Cas sighed and held out his hand to Lyzandor. The Earth house mage shook it. Cas said, "For the first time, I think we fully understand each other."

And maybe they did, but Rosalinde also understood them at that moment. They were two men she had hurt, two allies still holding onto pain from her actions, and she wasn't sure she could do anything to repair the damage that had been done.

Seventeen

L arkin did not have the Water house scouts. It was bad news.

"How did you know where to send your runner?" Ros asked.

"Observation," Larkin replied. "Lady Auguste feels secure with Air house outside our gates; it has the opposite effect on me. Their presence makes me nervous, so I've been paying more attention than ever. I spotted you when you shadow-walked them to the ridge. When I spotted Cassian meeting someone there three hours later, I dispatched Noah with a message."

"If you spotted us, Air house could have as well," Cassian said.

"When Noah came back with your message, he told me you asked about someone named Kaith. As soon as I heard the name, I shared it with my spies to keep an ear out. I'll let you know if we get a bite," Larkin said.

"What would you have us do in the meantime?" Zandor asked.

"Stay undetected," Cas said.

Ros nodded. "Secrecy is our best weapon. Stay quiet, listen for any information that could be helpful, and we'll be in touch."

"Send Noah here," Cassian said. "I'll relay information through him."

"He's terrified of you," Ros said.

Cas smiled. "That's what makes it fun."

"Noah it is," Larkin said.

As the group prepared to depart, Zandor gave Cas a nod and said, "Keep her safe."

"Always," Cas replied. With that, he took Rosalinde's hand, and the shadows took them.

$$\triangle$$

THE SHADOWS RECEDED as Ros and Cassian reappeared in Water house. Sapphire-colored drapes rustled softly with the breeze. The air inside was thick with the scent of old wood, burning oil, and the quiet hum of tension that had settled over them like a shroud. Cassian released her hand, and Ros took a moment to steady herself, letting the lingering rush of the shadow-walk slip away.

Cassian's eyes were already scanning the map spread out on the central table, the one they had pored over countless times. He was methodical, always looking for new angles, new opportunities to outmaneuver their enemies. Ros admired that about him, and how he never forgot about the people those strategies would affect.

Ros's thoughts, however, were still on the encounter in the stables. Larkin's offer to act as a spy within Earth house's court could tip the scales in their favor, but Ros couldn't shake the unease that gnawed at her. Trust was a fragile thing, especially now, and while she wanted to believe in Larkin and Lyzandor, the seeds of doubt had been sown.

"I don't like it," Cassian said, breaking the silence. His voice was calm, but there was an edge to it that Ros recognized all too well.

"You don't like what?" Ros asked, though she had a feeling she already knew the answer.

Cassian's gaze met hers, and there was a flicker of something—concern, perhaps—in his eyes. "Relying on Larkin and Lyzandor. It's too risky. We've seen what happens when trust is misplaced."

Ros crossed her arms, her mind replaying the conversation with the siblings. "We need them, Cas. Earth house is a stronghold, and if we can get inside their defenses, we'll have a better chance at taking down Air house's forces."

"And if they betray us?" Cassian asked, his voice low, almost a growl. "We can't afford to let our guard down."

Ros sighed, understanding his concerns but feeling the weight of her own decision. "I know the risks, but we have to take them. We're outnumbered, and we need every advantage we can get. If there's even a chance that Larkin and Lyzandor can help, we have to try."

Cassian was silent for a moment, his eyes searching hers. Finally, he nodded, though the tension in his posture remained. "Just promise me one thing."

"What's that?" she asked, her voice softening.

"If they give you any reason to doubt them—any reason at all—you won't hesitate to cut them loose. We can't let sentiment cloud our judgment."

Ros swallowed, knowing the truth in his words. "I promise."

Cassian gave a curt nod, seemingly satisfied with her answer, and turned his attention back to the map. "We'll need to hurry. If Larkin's right about Valeria's uncertainty, we have a narrow window to strike before she solidifies her alliances."

Ros moved to the table, her eyes scanning the familiar lines and markings that represented the terrain and fortifications around Earth house. "We should hit them from the east," she said, pointing to a narrow path that led to the less fortified side. "It's risky, but if we can get our forces through undetected, we'll have the element of surprise."

Cassian studied the map, his fingers tracing the route. "We'll need to move under the cover of darkness. I can shadow-walk a strike team ahead to secure the pass while the main force follows. We'll need Larkin and Lyzandor to ensure the gates are open when we arrive."

Ros nodded, feeling a flicker of hope amid the tension. "Alaric is already on the move with his forces. We need a solid plan in place before he gets there. This might be what puts the Air force soldiers in our grasp."

There was a quick rap on the door, barely long enough for Ros and Cas to turn their attention that way before Brisa strode in. She gave a quick nod of acknowledgement to Ros before turning her attention to Cassian.

"We've received word from Rowan," Brisa said, her voice steady but tinged with concern.

"Who is Rowan?" Ros asked.

Brisa looked back and forth between them, shook her head, and said, "Sorry."

Cassian raised his eyebrows at Brisa and they shared a look, at which point Brisa seemed to indicate that she would not be the one to tell Ros.

After watching the exchange, Ros said, "I really thought we were beyond secrets, at least within our inner circle."

"We are," Cassian said. "Mostly. There are still some secrets from Night house that I've been holding close. Old habits and all."

"So, Rowan is someone from your house, and you have them at Earth house reporting back."

"Like me, Rowan is a Shadow-walker. The best I've ever seen."

Brisa laughed. "That had to be painful to say. Admitting you're not the best at something is a rare thing."

Cas puckered his lips, giving her a flat look. "I can easily admit people are better at things when they are. But you are not better at cards, no matter how many claims you make."

"Don't you remember—"

"Apologies for the interruption," Ros cut in, "but what did shadow-walking Rowan have to report?"

Brisa winced. "Air House has sent reinforcements. He suspects they are going to attack Earth house outright."

"It doesn't make sense," Cas said. "Earth house has offered no opposition as Air house placed their troops in preparation of a Water house assault. Why would they march against a potential ally now?"

"Maybe they were never planning to attack Water house. They thought they had it under control with Graeme," Brisa said.

"So, they were planning to go after Earth house the whole time and no one realized it," Ros said.

"It makes sense," Cas said.

"Do you think Larkin and Zandor convinced Lady Auguste to side with us?" Ros asked.

"She may have already been leaning our way. Or maybe Air house is tired of waiting for her to decide. Either way, I'm sure she has made her decision now," Cassian said.

Ros thought of all the people at Earth house in danger from the onslaught headed their way, and her heart sank. She turned back to Brisa and asked, "How many soldiers?"

"Enough to make things difficult," she replied, her eyes dark. "If they reach Earth House before we do, we'll lose any advantage we have."

Cassian cursed under his breath, his hands clenched

into fists. "Alaric is already on the way, but they have the advantage if there are flight mages in their ranks."

Ros's mind raced, weighing their options. The timing was critical—if they moved too soon; they risked exposing their forces before Larkin and Lyzandor could secure their position and determine which side Earth house was going to support. But if they waited too long, the reinforcements would strengthen the enemy defenses beyond their ability to breach.

"We'll move at midday," Ros decided, her voice firm. "Waiting longer isn't an option. We'll find Alaric's troops and shadow-walk them a few at a time to the ridge near Earth house. Brisa, spread the word. Gather anyone who can move through the shadows. If they can only travel over short distances, plan a route to get them safely there in smaller trips."

Brisa nodded, her expression resolute. "I'll see to it."

As Brisa left the room, Ros turned back to Cassian, who was already adjusting their plans in his mind. She could see the gears turning, his strategic mind working through every possible scenario. He said, "We'll need to be careful."

Before he could speak further, Ros stepped toward him and said, "What is happening between us?"

His eyes went wide, as if that was the absolute last thing he expected from her. And maybe it was. They hadn't exactly had time for love and romance. Though both had expressed their feelings for each other, both had gone so far as to declare their love for one another, but the spark that had burned between them when they'd first met was barely an ember. Ros had begun to wonder if she was clinging to him as her future because she was afraid of what it would mean to be without the solidness that he offered. Now, to know he was still keeping secrets, she felt even more unsure of what she was really holding onto.

He stared at her in silence for a moment. "I meant what I said earlier," Cassian finally broke the silence, his voice steady but tinged with an emotion that made Ros's heart ache. "About how we need to be careful about the risks we're taking. But there's something else I need to say."

Ros turned to him, her eyes searching his face in the pale light coming through the window. "What is it?"

Cassian took a deep breath, his black eyes locking onto hers with an intensity that made her breath catch. "My feelings for you haven't changed. They've only grown stronger. But I've been holding back, keeping a distance because... because I don't want to complicate things when there's so much at stake."

Ros felt a lump form in her throat, her heart beating faster. "Cassian, I feel the same way. But we can't—"

"I know," he interrupted gently, his hand brushing against hers and trailing up her arm, sending a warm shiver through her. "Saving the kingdom has to come first. We have responsibilities, to our people, to our allies, to everyone who's depending on us. But that doesn't mean I've stopped loving you. What I hope is happening between us is that we're getting closer, we're learning more about one another, we're building a relationship that we can grow once this is all over."

Ros swallowed hard, the words catching in her throat. "But how can we think about a future when everything is so uncertain? We don't know if we'll even survive the next battle."

Cassian took her hand in his, his touch both grounding and electrifying. "That's why I need you to know that I meant what I said before, back in the woods. I told you I wouldn't kiss you until I knew you would spend the rest of your life kissing only me. I can't let myself fall fully in love with someone without knowing that. Because once I'm in, Ros, it's going to be forever. So yes, I love you, but I'm doing my damnedest to hold myself back from falling all the way."

Ros's heart ached at the memory, at the passion and restraint in his voice when he'd said those words before they'd fought Gaius that first time. It felt like so long ago, and they'd barely had time to think about such things since. "Everything has been so extreme, so chaotic... You're allowed to change your mind. If you aren't sure... Are you certain you still want me?"

"I do," Cassian said, a smile crawling across his face. "I meant every word. When this is over—when we've won this war and the kingdom is safe—I want to be with you, Ros. I want to spend the rest of my life making sure you know how much I love you."

Ros's breath caught, tears welling in her eyes as she stared at him, seeing the truth of his words reflected in his gaze. "I want that too, Cas. More than anything. But until then..."

"Until then," Cassian said, his voice softening as he brushed a strand of hair from her face, "we focus on saving the kingdom. We fight with everything we have. And when it's over, we'll have our time."

Ros closed her eyes, leaning into his touch as a tear slipped down her cheek. "I'm scared that something will happen, and we'll never get that chance."

Cassian cupped her cheek, wiping away the tear with his thumb. "Nothing's going to happen to us. I won't let it. We've come too far, and we're too strong together. We'll win this, and then we'll have the life we've both dreamed of."

Ros nodded, her heart swelling with a mix of hope and fear. "Promise me that no matter what happens, you'll hold on to that dream."

"I promise," Cassian whispered, his voice thick with emotion. "I promise to love you, to fight for you, and to be there when this is all over. We'll have our life together. I swear it."

Ros's tears flowed freely now, but she didn't care. She leaned in, resting her forehead against his, feeling the warmth of his breath against her skin, the steady beat of his heart beneath her hand.

"Thank you," she said, her voice trembling with the weight of all she felt. "For everything."

Cassian smiled, a soft, sad smile that spoke of all the

battles they had yet to fight, but also of the hope that they would one day win. "Always."

For a long moment, they sat there in silence, the world around them fading away as they held onto each other, drawing strength from the bond they shared. The storm was coming, but at this moment, they were together, and that was enough.

When they finally pulled away, Cas gave her a half smile and said, "Go get some rest. I'll have someone wake you when it's close to midday."

"I don't think I could sleep if I wanted to."

"You need to. We both do if we're going to be of use to anyone."

Ros nodded, and they walked out of the room hand in hand. Cassian grabbed a passing servant in the corridor and told them to wake them before the lunch meal was served, then he shadow-walked them to Rosalinde's room. He kissed Ros on the forehead and released her as if to leave, but Ros clung to his tunic and said, "Stay."

So he did.

Eighteen

Ros stirred slightly, the warmth of the midday sun filtering through the thin fabric of her bedroom curtains and casting a soft, golden light over the space. She snuggled deeper into the comfort of the blankets, the steady rhythm of Cassian's heartbeat beneath her ear a soothing lullaby that made her feel safe, even with the weight of the world pressing down on them.

Cassian's arm was draped protectively around her waist, his breath gentle against her hair as he slept. It was a rare moment of peace, one that Ros cherished more than anything else in these turbulent times. For just a few hours, the outside world, with all its dangers and uncertainties, could be forgotten.

But that peace was abruptly shattered when Ros lifted her gaze and found her sister standing at the foot of the bed. She stared at them, arms crossed over her chest, and said, "This is not how I wanted to find my sister today."

Ros rolled her eyes. "We were just sleeping."

"Right," Elsa said with a smirk.

Cassian stirred awake, blinking sleepily as he realized what was happening. A slow, mischievous smile spread across his face as he tightened his hold on Ros, making no effort to move away. "Good morning, Elsabet," he drawled, clearly amused by the situation.

Elsa grimaced. "Gross."

Ros, still flustered, sat up, though Cassian's arm remained securely around her waist. "What did you need, Elsa?" she asked, trying to sound composed but failing miserably.

"It's almost midday," Elsa said. "Brisa has a collection of shadowy figures waiting in the war room, and they're making people nervous. We need to get going."

Cassian chuckled, the sound low and warm. "We'll be out in a moment. And next time, you should really knock. You never know what you might walk in on."

Ros shot him a glare, though the corner of her mouth twitched with amusement. "Cas, stop. You're going to give her the wrong impression."

"You act as if Elsabet doesn't have her own love life to contend with," he said.

A mischievous glint appeared in Rosalinde's eyes as she said, "Oh, that's right. How are things with Brisa?"

Elsa's eyes widened, a blush creeping up her neck. "What do you mean?"

Cassian leaned back, crossing his arms over his chest as

he grinned at Elsa. "Oh, come on, Elsa. We've all seen the way you two look at each other."

"Brisa and I are just... friends."

"Sure you are," Ros teased. "That's exactly what it sounded like when she was describing her... needs. And why she keeps finding excuses to be around you."

Elsa opened her mouth to protest, but the words seemed to die in her throat. "I... I don't know what you're talking about."

Cassian raised an eyebrow. "Really? Because Brisa was asking about you just the other day."

Elsa's eyes widened. "And?"

Ros said, "And if you're interested—which we all know you are—you should talk to her."

Elsa bit her lip. "There's too much going on to worry about that, too."

Cassian said, "We've all got a lot to fight for. But you can't waste the time you have waiting for the perfect moment that may never come."

"I guess that's why I found you here," Elsa said.

"Maybe," Cas shrugged. "Or maybe I just couldn't stand to be away from your sister for another minute."

Elsabet grimaced and said, "That's enough sharing for now. I'll see you in the hall in ten minutes."

And with that, Elsa departed, and they settled back into the warmth of each other's embrace.

ROS MOVED through the quiet corridors of the castle, her footsteps barely audible against the stone floors. The scent of herbs and faint smoke lingered in the air, a sign that the healing wing was close. She rubbed her arms as she walked, her mind racing with thoughts of the battle behind them—and the uncertain future ahead. *Queen*. The word felt heavy on her shoulders, a weight she wasn't sure she was ready to carry.

When she had accepted the role the first time, it was because she didn't have a choice. Her father was missing, and the only way to keep the throne from falling into the wrong hands was to assume the position herself. Now her father was back and could return to his place if he wished. Despite the protests of Cassian, Alaric, and Darian, before his demise, staying in power wasn't as easy a task as they wanted. It wasn't an evil ruler they were trying to depose, it was her *father*. He was kind, he tried to be fair, and he wanted to serve the people of Talabrih—he just didn't do things the way the others wanted. The way *she* wanted, if she was being honest. Still, she had to talk to him and figure out how this should work and what she should do.

As she turned a corner, she spotted Teague up ahead, bent over a patient's bed. His hands moved deftly, tending to a wound that looked nearly healed, his brow furrowed in concentration. Beckett stood beside him, a calming presence, quietly passing him tools and murmuring words of comfort to the injured.

"Ros," Teague called out, noticing her before she could make her way past. He gave her a warm smile, though fatigue was etched in his features. "I didn't think we'd see you here. Everyone thought you'd be taking some time to rest."

She returned his smile, though it didn't reach her eyes. "Rest seems far away right now. I came to see my father."

Beckett, ever the more observant of the two, gave her a knowing look. "The crown weighing heavy already?"

Ros nodded, biting her lip. "More than I thought it would."

Teague wiped his hands clean and came to stand beside her. "We're all glad you made it through the battle. Earth House took a beating, but we did what we had to."

"We did," Ros agreed, her gaze drifting toward the window where rays of sunlight filtered through. The scars of the battle still haunted her. She turned back to Teague and Beckett, offering a small, grateful smile. "I'm glad you both made it through, too. I don't know what I'd do if... if we lost any more of us."

Beckett placed a comforting hand on her shoulder. "We're still here, and we'll keep fighting with you. Together. You're not alone in this, Ros."

She nodded, a wave of relief washing over her at his words. "Thank you. Both of you."

Teague gave her a gentle nudge, gesturing toward the end of the hall. "Your father's in the back room. He's been asking about you between patients. I think he's worried you're carrying too much on your own."

Asking about me, but not willing to come and see me himself? she thought. Ros swallowed, the weight of what she needed to discuss with him settling more heavily in her chest. "Maybe I am. I just don't know how to carry it yet."

With a final glance at Teague and Beckett, she continued down the hall, passing through the threshold into the quiet chamber where her father rested. The room smelled faintly of lavender and chamomile, a Healer's touch in the atmosphere. Her father, the once mighty king, stood at the bedside of a fallen mage who was recovering thanks to the medics of Water house. Tancred looked thinner than she remembered, his hair streaked with more silver than before.

His eyes lit up when he saw her, a tired smile spreading across his face. "My darling," he said, voice soft but full of affection. "It's good to see you."

She smiled, his presence offering her a bit of peace. Ros had visited her father in the medical wing many times over the years, and the sight of him here reminded her of how things were just a month ago. For a moment, the weight of her title and duties slipped away, and she was simply his daughter again.

"Let's walk," he said, taking her by the hand and leading her out of the room. They walked slowly down the corridor, Ros comforted by the confidence of her father in his element.

"I need your advice," she admitted, her voice trembling despite herself. "I don't know how to do this. How to be queen. I don't even know where to start."

He sighed, squeezing her hand gently. "No one ever truly knows, not at first. You learn as you go, just as I did. But, if

I'm honest..." He paused, his expression becoming wistful. "I never wanted this life for you. If I could have chosen, I would never have been king. I would have been a healer."

Ros blinked, taken aback by the admission. "I know you love healing, and you spent much of your time here, but are you saying you wouldn't have served Talabrih if you had the choice?"

He nodded slowly, eyes drifting toward the herbs hanging from the walls. "I've always had a love for healing. It was my dream before I ever wore the crown. I could have spent a happy life away from politics, but duty called, and I answered. As you must now."

Ros felt a lump in her throat as she absorbed his words. "You were a good king. Strong. Wise."

"That's kind of you," he said with a faint smile. "But recent events have shown me I wasn't who this kingdom needed. I tried, but it wasn't enough. My heart was never truly in it, and it showed. And that's something I hope you'll keep in mind, Ros. You can be queen, yes, but never forget who you are at your core. Lead as yourself, not the version of you that others demand. I could have healed Talabrih, in a fashion, but I didn't and I regret it."

She looked down at their intertwined hands, her father's words echoing in her mind. "I don't know what I can offer."

"You will figure it out," he said softly. "You just have to give yourself time to find yourself. Fortunately, you have some good people by your side to help you."

Ros nodded, the weight on her chest easing slightly. "Thank you."

His smile deepened, a spark of the strength she remembered in his eyes. "I'll always be here for you. Whatever happens."

With a final squeeze of his hand, she nodded and said her goodbye, feeling a little more grounded than she had when she first entered. As she left the healing wing, her mind was clearer, her heart a little steadier. Maybe she didn't know how to be queen yet, but she had the people she loved, and they would help her carry the weight.

Ros pushed open the heavy doors of the war room, Cassian immediately at her side when she entered. The tension in the air was palpable, the kind that preceded a storm—or a battle. Brisa and Elsa were already there, standing close together by the large map spread across the table. Around them, six shadowy figures loomed—silent, almost blending into the dim light. These were the Shadow-walkers, their presence more felt than seen.

Brisa nodded in greeting, her eyes sharp. "You're just in time. We were beginning to discuss the plan."

Elsa looked up from the map. "Cassian, I believe you know the Shadow-walkers."

"I do," he said.

One of the Shadow-walkers, a tall, lithe figure in his late thirties, with long silver hair pulled into a low ponytail, and a voice like rustling leaves, stepped forward. "We are ready to serve. As it has been explained by Lady Brisa, our task is to shadow-walk your army to the ridge of Earth house before the Air house reinforcements arrive."

Cassian glanced at the map, then at Ros. "Yes. Once we're on the crest, we'll have the high ground, but we'll also be exposed. We need to be ready for anything."

"How long do we have?"

"Not long. Air house is already on the way."

"How far can you each travel at once?" Ros asked.

The tall man said, "I can get to Earth house without an issue."

Cas smiled. "Queen Rosalinde, this is Rowan, the Night mage I told you about."

"The one who is better than you at shadow-walking," Ros said, offering Rowan a smile.

With a smirk, Rowan said, "I'd wager I'm better at a lot of things, Your Majesty. You let me know if you want to find out for yourself."

Rosalinde's brows shot up, but Cassian stepped between them and ushered Ros to the next Night mage. She was very much the opposite of Rowan, with short swooping hair that hung towards amethyst eyes, an eager smile, and shadows practically rolling off her short, curvy figure. Cas said, "This is Cressida. Another powerhouse Night mage."

"Pleasure," Ros said.

Cressida smiled up at Ros and said, "The pleasure is all mine, Queen Rosalinde. And, for the record, I'm also better than Lord Cassian at most things."

"Good grief," Cassian muttered, pressing a finger against the crease between his eyes.

"And you two," Ros said, smiling at the next Night mages. "I assume you make Cassian seem like an amateur at all things."

"Naturally," the girl said. She shot Ros a grin and held out her hand. "I'm Indigo, and this is my brother, Eryx."

"Twins," he said, taking Rosalinde's hand in turn.

Cassian asked, "What is wrong with you all? I bring you to meet the queen of Talabrih, and this is how you repay me?"

With a shrug, Brisa said, "This is why we can't have nice things."

"What did you expect from us when you introduced us to this tall drink of Water house?" Cressida asked, waving a hand toward Rosalinde

"You're right," Cas said. "I should have known better."

One of the last Shadow-walkers, a person with shaggy brown curls and startling green eyes, said, "At least I'm here to balance things out. My shadow-walking is much shorter distance, and my grasp of the darkness is tentative at best. So, I'm not better at most things."

"Thank you, Sage," Cas replied.

Sage smiled. "No problem. I'm happy to admit that I'm only better than you at the more fun, intimate things. But shadow-walking is all you, Lord Cassian."

Ros laughed heartily and looked around at the mages all smiling back at her. It was clear they had a great relationship with Cassian, their lord, and were willing to extend that to her as well. It felt great to be part of that, to share in their fun, even if only for a brief respite before they returned to the turmoil of what was to come. Maybe this was their way of coping with the fact that war was on their doorstep.

She turned to the last of the Shadow-walkers. He was young, only thirteen or fourteen, if she was guessing. Ros stepped in front of him and asked, "And you are?"

"Your future king, if you'll get rid of this guy."

The room erupted in laughter. Cassian faced the kid and said, "You too, Bastian?"

Bastian's face broke out in a huge grin. "Apologies, Lord Cassian, but Rowan gave me five coppers to say it."

Cassian wrapped his arm around Bastian's neck and pulled him close, rustling his hair. "You're lucky Queen Rosalinde is in such a good mood from spending time with me, or she'd have you all quartered."

"No, she wouldn't," Brisa said. "Our queen is good."

"That's high praise coming from you," Cressida said.

Brisa said, "I mean it. She wants the best for all of us. I, for one, am privileged to serve her."

"All of us will share that privilege soon enough. When do we leave?" Rowan asked.

"Now," Brisa said. "We'll go together to Chambron village, where Alaric is waiting for us. Once we leave there, Sage and Bastian, you're with me. We're going to walk shorter distances to stave off the exhaustion. The others can make the bigger treks on their own."

Bastian and Sage moved to Brisa's sides, forcing Elsa to

take a step back. She looked as if she wanted to say something to Brisa before they set off, but instead she turned away and faced her sister.

"We're counting on you. If we can engage the Air house force before their reinforcements arrive, we have a chance to turn Earth house. Until Air house backs down, we'll never be able to resolve the rest of the mess that Gaius and Graeme caused."

Ros took a deep breath, meeting each of their gazes. "Then let's not waste any more time. We have a kingdom to save."

THE AIR in Chambron was still, the sun casting a golden light over the small village where Alaric's army rested. The Shadow-walkers materialized in the nearby woods, silent and swift as a stone plummeting through water.

Ros stepped forward to the edge of the village where Alaric paced, her presence instantly calming the tension that had been building. Cassian was beside her, his movements fluid and deliberate. Brisa followed close behind, a quiet intensity in her gaze, with Sage, Rowan, Cressida, Bastian, Eryx, and Indigo fanning out around them like the edges of a dark star.

Alaric met Ros's eyes, his expression a mixture of relief and determination. "You made it," he said, his voice low but firm. "The men are ready. They'll follow your lead."

"How are they?" she asked, concern etched on her face.

"Resolute," he said. "Scared. As ready as they're going to get."

Ros nodded, glancing back at the Shadow-walkers. "We don't have much time. The Air house reinforcements could arrive at any moment."

Cassian stepped forward, his words like a whisper in the night. "We'll move them through the shadows. It'll be disorienting for some, but they'll arrive quickly and unseen."

Rowan added, "Tell them to stay close and not to panic."

Alaric turned to his men, raising his voice so all could hear. "Listen up! We're moving with the Shadow-walkers. Stay close, stay quiet, and trust them to lead us. We fight for our kingdom, and today, we take the first step."

They murmured their assent, their faces hardening with resolve. Brisa, Sage, and Cressida moved among them, offering quiet words of encouragement as they grouped the soldiers together, while Indigo and Eryx stood watch, their eyes never leaving the edges of the village. Bastian, the smallest of the group but no less formidable, took his place near the rear, ready to guide the stragglers.

Ros met Alaric's gaze once more. "Let's move out. We'll take them to the ridge, and from there, we fight."

Without another word, the Shadow-walkers took hands with the groups near them and enveloped them in darkness. The air grew cool, the sounds of the village fading as the shadows deepened. One by one, the soldiers vanished into the night, swallowed by the Shadow-walkers' power.

Ros felt the familiar tug of the darkness as it drew her forward, guiding her steps through the inky blackness. Alaric was close beside her, clinging to her hand, his presence a talisman that kept her on the path. They moved quickly, the world around them a blur of shapes and fleeting light.

And then, as suddenly as they had entered the in-between place, they emerged on the ridge of Earth house. The soldiers appeared behind them, shaken but ready, their eyes scanning the horizon for the first signs of the enemy.

Ros looked back at the Shadow-walkers, already disappearing back to Chambron to gather more soldiers. She let go of Alaric's hand and said, "I'll be right back."

"Rosa, wait," he said.

She looked at him, but his eyes were cast toward Earth house and the trees beyond. She could see the forest to the west moving. Not like a breeze blowing through, but like a great turbulence passed them, pulling some of them out of the very ground.

"It's too late," she said. "They're already here."

Alaric cursed under his breath, his hand tightening around the hilt of his sword. "They've beaten us here. We're outnumbered."

Ros surveyed the enemy's ranks, her mind racing. "We can't take them head-on. Not like this."

Cassian stepped forward, his eyes narrowing. "They don't know we're here yet. We can stay hidden and wait until nightfall to use the shadows."

Alaric shook his head. "That'll only help with a few soldiers, not a whole army."

Rowan appeared again, another group of soldiers in tow. He ushered them into the nearby woods and turned as if to leave again until he spotted Ros, Cassian, and Alaric muttering and pointing at the distant tree line. He sidled up beside them and said, "Already here?" Cas nodded and Rowan asked, "Nighttime shadow attack?"

"Not with the full army," Alaric said.

"Of course not," Rowan said. "That would be foolish. We split our forces. A small group infiltrates the Air house camp and causes enough chaos to disrupt their lines. The rest of the army will position themselves for a surprise attack from the ridge."

Cas nodded slowly. "If we strike at their leaders or take out key positions, we could weaken their command before they realize what's happening."

Ros considered the idea, her gaze shifting to the Shadow-walkers depositing soldiers a few at a time. "That could work, but we need more than a distraction. We need to sow confusion and keep them guessing about our numbers."

Cassian said, "We Shadow-walkers can move between their ranks, spread fear. We don't need to fight directly— we just need them to think there's a larger force than what's really here."

Alaric chimed in. "Meanwhile, we can take control of the high ground and cut off their retreat. If they believe they're surrounded, we'll have the advantage. And if we position archers along the ridge, we can rain arrows down on them once the chaos starts. It could break their ranks."

"Any word from Kaith or the scouts? They could have information that would help us," Brisa asked, joining the group.

"Not for a few hours," Cas said. "They could be lying low..."

His voice trailed off, but they all heard the unspoken words: or she could be dead.

Ros exhaled slowly, feeling the weight of the decision. "Alright. Here's the plan: Cassian and I will lead the infiltration team. We'll shadow-walk in with Rowan, Eryx, Indigo, and Cressida, and target their leaders. Bastian, Sage, and Brisa will stay here in case things go sideways and they need to start moving people away from the battlefield. Alaric, coordinate the archers on the ridge and position the rest of the army to strike once the confusion sets in."

Everyone nodded, the urgency of the situation pushing aside any hesitation.

"We'll have one chance at this," Ros continued. "If we fail, Earth house falls. But if we succeed, we can push them back and take control of the field."

Alaric's eyes gleamed with determination. "Then let's make sure we don't fail."

WITH ALL PLANS IN PLACE, the day wore on as the groups made their final preparations. Ros moved among her commanders, offering words of encouragement and ensuring everyone knew their roles. The tension was palpable, each person acutely aware of the stakes.

As midnight approached, the first signs of movement emerged. Under the cover of darkness, the Shadow-walkers led their groups towards their targets. Ros stood at the forefront, her heart pounding with a mixture of fear and determination.

"Remember," she called out quietly, addressing her troops, "we fight not just for ourselves, but for the future of our kingdom. Stay focused, stay strong."

With a final breath, Ros gave the signal, and the assault began.

Nineteen

The night air was thick with anticipation as Ros gave the signal. In an instant, the Shadow-walkers melted into the darkness. The world blurred into shadowy silence, their movements swift and soundless. Time felt distorted within the shadows, but Ros kept her focus, the weight of the kingdom's future driving her forward.

They emerged on the outskirts of the Air house camp, unseen and unheard. Fires burned low in the center of the camp, casting flickering light over the enemy soldiers, unaware of the danger creeping toward them. Ros scanned the site for signs of leadership—the command tent, where their enemies' most vital decisions were made.

"There," Cassian whispered, pointing toward a large tent draped with Air house insignia.

Ros nodded, motioning for the others to spread out. "Remember the plan," she murmured. "We strike fast and hard, take out the leaders, and slip back into the shadows before they realize what hit them."

Rowan, Eryx, and Indigo fanned out to cover the perimeter, while Cressida stayed close to Ros and Cassian. With a silent signal, they moved toward the command tent.

Inside, the Air house commanders gathered, their voices low but confident. Ros crept closer, her heart pounding as she glimpsed their target: a tall man with silver hair and a cold, calculating presence—one of Air house's most ruthless nobles and the Lord Ruler's brother, Eamon Barclay. There could be no doubt about Hessian's involvement now, not that there ever truly was.

Ros steeled herself, her grip tightening on her weapon. This was their moment.

Suddenly, a sharp cry pierced the silence—a sentry had spotted them. The camp erupted into chaos. Soldiers scrambled to arms, and shouts echoed through the night.

"Now!" Ros hissed, and they charged.

Cassian threw a wave of dark magic, sending a surge of energy toward the general, but he was fast, deflecting it with a shield of air. The magic crackled against the invisible barrier, sparks flying. The air between them thickened with tension, the ground trembling beneath their feet from the sheer force of the magic.

Ros darted in, a spear of fire aimed for Eamon Barclay. He parried with his gift, his eyes flashing with fury, and the two engaged in a swift, brutal duel. Each strike was a deadly dance, Ros's flames licking through the air as the commander spun, weaving gusts of wind that fanned the fire into a deadly storm.

The general swung his blade, sharp and gleaming, cutting through the air with a whistle. Ros narrowly dodged, the blade skimming her arm as she pivoted, launching a water attack toward him. The wave hit the ground, leaving a pit of mud in the middle of the space, but Eamon kicked up a vortex of air, spinning his own arc back toward her.

Cassian, seeing Ros under pressure, hurled a tendril of shadows, attempting to bind the general's legs. The darkness coiled like a serpent, but the commander twisted, sending a whirlwind to dispel the shadows just as Ros lunged with her spear of air. It clashed against his sword, the impact ringing through the camp.

Their weapons locked for a moment, and Eamon's sneer deepened. "You think your power can match my wind?" he growled, pushing back with an explosive burst of wind that sent Ros stumbling.

Cassian surged forward, his hands crackling with dark energy. He unleashed a barrage of shadows that clawed at the air, twisting like living creatures. The general was forced to redirect his attention, whirling to deflect the onslaught. Dark magic collided with wind in a brilliant explosion, sending both men staggering back, but the general recovered first.

Ros took the opportunity, her eyes blazing with fury. She called upon the full force of her magic, and flames erupted from her hands, burning hotter, brighter than before. With a furious cry, she hurled the firestorm toward the commander. He raised his hand to block it, but the fire surged through his defenses, engulfing him in a fiery whirlwind.

He screamed in pain, his shield of air crumbling as he was driven to his knees. Cassian, seizing the moment, sent another blast of shadows, this time striking true. Barclay gasped, his body seized by the dark tendrils, his struggles weakening as the magic overwhelmed him.

Finally, Ros stepped forward, her spear poised, flames still dancing along its length. She looked down at the fallen commander, their eyes locking for a brief, intense moment. "Graeme is dead," she said. "It's time to end this."

A smile peeled across his face. "The boy was just one of many tools to use against the throne. We will not stop until your tyranny is over."

Ros stepped back at his words. *Tyranny. Is that truly how it felt to the people of Air house?*

Cassian, sensing the battle around them slipping, called out to Ros. "We need to retreat! Our team is outnumbered."

Ros gritted her teeth, still staring down at the commander. "Not yet!"

"You won't do it," Eamon said. "You don't have the stomach for killing."

Rosalinde's fist clenched around her weapon, and she snarled, "Who do you think killed Graeme Monsanato?"

There was a flash of surprise on Barclay's face. Ros relished the look. Still, his surprise didn't matter—Ros was out of time. More soldiers flooded the camp, the odds turned against them. Ros looked up to see Eryx staggering back, injured, while Rowan barely deflected a spear aimed at his side. They were overwhelmed.

Ros stabbed a spear of air into the ground in front of her. While she had distractedly watched her allies in near-misses, Eamon had snuck away. "Damn it," she growled. "Where did he go?"

She spun around but didn't see him. He was lost in the chaos of the approaching soldiers. Just as it seemed they might be overrun, the signal horn blared from the ridge. Alaric and his archers had begun their assault, arrows raining down on the Air house soldiers below. Panic spread through the base as the encamped army was caught off guard by the sudden onslaught.

"Fall back!" Ros shouted, slicing her way through a pair of advancing soldiers. "Into the shadows."

Cassian unleashed a burst of magic, pushing back the enemy, and together, they retreated, fading back into the darkness just as they had come. The world blurred again as they were pulled through the shadows, leaving the camp in disarray behind them.

They emerged near the ridge where Bastian, Sage, and Brisa were waiting, ready to move the remaining troops if necessary.

Ros doubled over, catching her breath, her heart still racing. "We didn't take out the commander," she said, her voice tight with frustration. "But we've created enough confusion for Alaric's forces to strike."

Cassian nodded, wiping the sweat from his brow. "We'll have to fight harder from here, but at least we've shaken their ranks."

The distant sound of clashing steel and the cries of battle filled the air. The real fight was just beginning. Ros straightened, her eyes fierce with resolve. "Then let's push forward. This is ours to win."

As Ros and the Shadow-walkers regrouped near the ridge, the sounds of war still raging below, something shifted in the air. The earth itself seemed to hum, a deep resonance that Ros felt in her bones. She straightened, glancing at Cassian, who had also noticed the change.

Before anyone could speak, the ground beneath them rumbled slightly, and from the shadows of the hillside emerged a group of figures draped in earthen-colored robes. Their movements were deliberate and powerful, each step causing the land to shift subtly, as if the earth itself responded to their presence. At the forefront was a lovely brown-skinned woman with sharp eyes and a staff in hand—Valeria Auguste, the ruler of Earth house.

Beside her were Larkin and Zandor, and just behind them, Kaith and two other scouts stood amongst the mages who joined them.

Ros stepped forward, her heart pounding wildly. "Larkin," she breathed, relief flooding her. "You found our scouts."

Larkin nodded. "They were detained."

"By Air house infiltrators," Kaith cut in. "We were able to slip them, but we had to hide and wait. Then word came around that the Earth house nobles were looking for us."

"Which, of course, was not an enticing thought since they didn't know which side we were on," Larkin said.

"We've been watching, waiting for a chance to come to you without ending up in Air house's camp instead. But Lady Zolto herself came to find me and explained what was happening. I'm sure you already know she can be quite convincing."

"Perhaps a bit too persuasive," Valeria cut in. "Because I am here now, and not sure I should be."

"How can I assure you?" Ros asked.

Valeria pursed her lips. "Truthfully, the moment Earth house became occupied by another house's forces, my decision was made. I do not always agree with the throne, but I know your father would have never allowed this to happen to my people, and they guarantee me you wouldn't either."

Larkin smiled and said, "We're here to help. Air house might have our city under siege, but the land still answers to us."

Zandor gave a chuckle. "We weren't about to let the Air house scum claim what's ours without a fight. Air house thinks they hold us hostage, but they do not know the power that runs through these lands."

Cassian looked between them, a spark of hope returning to his eyes. "What can you do to help?"

Valeria raised her staff, the ground trembling slightly beneath them. "The earth is our ally. We can manipulate the terrain, use it to trap their forces, and strengthen your defenses. We've already weakened their foundations so that pits are opening under them even now."

Zandor smirked, his hands flexing, as if eager to get to work. "Let us deal with their camp. We'll make sure it becomes a deathtrap."

Cassian said, "If you can push them away from the gates, Alaric's archers are already in position and can take them out. When the ammunition is gone, we'll move in for hand to hand."

Ros took a deep breath, feeling the weight of the moment settle on her shoulders. But with the Earth mages at their side, the odds were shifting in their favor. "Alright," she said, her voice steady. "Let's strike from both sides. Valeria, you and your mages weaken their defenses. Cassian and I will lead the charge from the ridge. We'll push the Air house forces into the traps you've laid."

Zandor grinned, already eager to begin. "This will be fun."

Valeria raised her hands, her voice a soft whisper as she called on the earth. The ground beneath them trembled in response, the stones and soil ready to bend to her will. Larkin and Zandor joined her, their powers building in harmony, and soon the land began to undulate.

The distant sound of crumbling stone echoed through the valley. Ros saw Air house soldiers stumble as rocks and dirt shifted beneath their feet.

Cassian's hand tightened on his sword as he turned to Ros. "This is our chance. Let's finish this."

Ros raised her hand, signaling the charge. Alaric's

forces surged forward from the ridge, arrows flying as they descended on the now-disoriented Air house troops.

With the Earth mages' power tearing through the enemy's defenses and their own army pressing from all sides, Earth house was no longer a fortress for the enemy— it was a battleground where the earth itself fought alongside them.

And Ros knew they would not fail.

Twenty

The sky above Earth house was choked with smoke and the metallic scent of battle. Air house soldiers scrambled as the land shifted beneath them, their ranks breaking apart. Arrows rained down from the ridge, and in the chaos, Ros led the charge from the high ground, her sword gleaming under the moonlight.

Behind her, Alaric's archers took careful aim, releasing volley after volley into the confusion below. Shadow-walkers darted between the ranks of the enemy, their dark cloaks blending with the night as they struck fast and vanished before Air house soldiers could retaliate.

The earth itself was coming alive under the control of the Earth mages. Lady Valeria, standing with Zandor and Larkin, had thrust her staff into the ground, her eyes glowing with power. With every gesture, the land obeyed—cracking open beneath the feet of enemy soldiers, throwing them off balance. Massive boulders broke free from the hillsides, rolling into the camp and crushing the opposition's fortifications. Soldiers screamed as the earth swallowed them whole or trapped them in fissures that opened without warning.

"Keep the pressure on them!" Ros shouted, her voice cutting through the din of the battle. She moved with precision, slicing through any soldier who dared to approach. Cassian was beside her, his shadows striking efficiently, deadly energy barely restrained as they moved through the battle.

Though the tide had turned in their favor, the battle was far from won. In the distance, near the heart of the fortress, Ros caught sight of the Air house general they had failed to kill earlier. His silver hair gleamed under the firelight as he shouted commands, rallying his troops. Ros cursed under her breath. The man was too skilled a tactician to let his forces be overwhelmed without a fight.

"We need to take him down," Ros said, turning to Cassian. "If he regains control of his army, they'll regroup."

Cassian nodded, his grip tightening on the hilt of his blade. "Leave him to me."

Without hesitation, Cassian darted toward the general, weaving through the battlefield with the agility of a Shadow-walker. Ros trusted him to finish what they had started, her focus turning back to her own fight. She pushed deeper into the enemy lines, cutting her way toward the heart of the camp where the remaining Air house troops were attempting to regroup.

At that moment, a deafening crack split the air, and the

ground beneath Earth house shifted violently. The battlements of Air house trembled, and in an instant, part of the outer wall crumbled into a heap of rubble. Zandor had directed his power into a final strike; furious screams echoed across the valley as the once impenetrable walls of Earth house fell.

"They're breaking," Alaric called from his position atop the ridge. His voice carried over the battlefield, rallying their troops. "Push forward."

With the Air house soldiers in disarray and their fortifications crumbling, Ros felt victory within reach. She led her forces in a last charge, her sword raised high as she shouted, "For the kingdom!"

The clash of steel rang out as Ros and her soldiers met the last of the Air house troops in fierce combat. Despite their numbers, the Air house forces were exhausted and demoralized. Their defenses were crumbling, and their leadership was faltering. The ground beneath their feet betrayed them at every turn, shifting and buckling as the Earth mages continued their assault.

Ros fought with every ounce of strength she had, her blade cutting through the chaos and magic shooting from her fingertips as she made her way to the heart of the battle. As she clashed, she caught sight of Cassian near the command tent, locked in a fierce duel with the silver-haired general. The two men moved like lightning, their blades flashing in the firelight as they clashed. Each man shot magic at the other, but they were too skilled for either to let the other's strikes land.

Cassian fought with a cold fury, his movements precise and unrelenting. He didn't speak, his focus entirely on his opponent.

Ros saw the danger he was in before he did. A soldier had snuck up on him and, blade extended, swung for Cassian's back.

"No!" she screamed, throwing out her hand toward the attacker.

A bolt of air shot from her hand, sending Cassian, Barclay, and the soldier flying. She saw Cassian land with a thud, and he did not rise. Ros shadow-walked the distance to them. Cassian's blade lay abandoned on the ground; Ros took it in her hand, adjusting to the feel of the grip. She turned in time to see Eamon Barclay rise.

With a swift strike, Ros disarmed the general, her blade at the man's throat in an instant.

"It's over," she said, her voice low and dangerous.

The general's eyes flashed with defiance, but he made no move to resist. Ros did not hesitate this time as she plunged the sword into the commander. She shifted her attention to the next enemy in her path until she finally cleared the area around Cassian.

Ros knelt beside him. His breathing was shallow but present. Cassian opened his eyes and gave Ros a faint smile. "Did you...?"

Ros nodded. "He's taken care of. Now I'm going to find you a Healer."

"No," he whispered, taking hold of her wrist. "You do it."

"I don't know how."

"It's in your blood," he said, a bout of coughing racking his body. "There's no time to find someone else."

Ros swallowed back her fear. She knew where the magic lived inside her, knew how to access it. She could do this.

Placing her hands on Cassian's midsection, Ros closed her eyes and reached for the elements flowing in her. She let her senses sort through the strands of power until she felt an unfamiliar one brush up against her mind. Ros pulled at the power, and when she was certain it was the right one, she pushed it into Cassian with all her might. She let the magic radiate through her, intertwined with the love she felt for this man. He could not die.

When she felt Cassian's hand on hers, Ros opened her eyes. He smiled up at her, his breathing returned to normal.

"Let's help you up," Rowan said, reaching down for his Night house lord.

Ros looked up to see that she and Cassian were surrounded by the Shadow-walkers. They had stood their ground around their lord and their queen, a ring of protection while Ros healed him.

They rose and looked around the battlefield. With their general defeated and their defenses shattered, the remaining Air house forces were surrendering. One by one, they dropped their weapons, raising their hands in submission. The camp grew quiet, the cries of battle fading as the dust settled over the land surrounding Earth house.

Ros stood in the center of the ruins, her breath heavy but steady. Ait house's forces were subdued, and Earth house had forged an alliance with them that, hopefully, would last well beyond tonight's battle. They had done it.

The Earth mages approached, their faces lined with exhaustion but filled with satisfaction. "The earth is quiet now," Valeria said, her voice a low rumble. "Earth house is ours again."

Alaric, his armor dented and scratched, approached from the ridge, his eyes gleaming with pride. "We couldn't have done it without you," he said to Ros.

Ros shook her head, a small smile tugging at her lips. "We did it together."

Rosalinde's gaze turned to the horizon, where the first light of dawn was breaking through the smoke-filled sky. They had won the battle, but the war was far from over. The shadow of war still loomed over the future of their kingdom.

But for now, they had Earth house as an ally, and they had friends to move forward to make Talabrih a better home for everyone. For now, they had hope.

Ros turned to her allies, her voice steady as she said, "We prepare for the next fight. This isn't over, but we'll keep going until we've won every last battle. We will be victorious."

Ros, Cassian, and their companions stepped through the massive gates of Earth house, greeted by a wave of sound that rose from the streets in front of them. Every path was alive, not only with people, but with life itself. Everywhere Ros looked, vibrant flora had sprung up from the rich earth—flowers in every hue, twisting vines that curled along stone walls, and towering trees that cast cool, dappled shade over the cobbled paths. The beauty was undeniable, but so too was the weight of the moment.

As they walked through the streets toward the heart of the city, people lined up on either side. Some cheered, their faces alight with hope. Men and women, young and old, waved banners with the symbol of Earth house emblazoned in green and gold, shouting their joy and relief at seeing their fortress retaken. Children darted through the crowd, chasing one another between the clusters of flowers that bloomed along the road.

Ros's heart swelled at the sight. They had endured so much. They had lived in fear of the Air house's occupation, of their growing reach. And now, for the first time in months, maybe years, for some of them, they could believe in something better.

But not all were celebrating. As Ros walked through the throngs of cheering people, she noticed others, quieter, standing in the shadows of the grand trees. Some cried, their faces streaked with tears as they clutched each other for support. She could see the grief etched into their expressions—angst for the loved ones they had lost, for the homes destroyed, for the scars that war had left on their hearts.

Cassian, walking beside her, noticed it too. "They've sacrificed so much," he murmured, his voice low. "Even with Earth house free, the cost is still fresh for them."

Ros nodded, her throat tightening as she looked out over the crowd. "We have a long road ahead. Reclaiming Earth house was just the beginning."

As they moved deeper into the city, the flora around them became more abundant, as if the earth itself were rejoicing in their victory. Brilliant flowers with petals that shimmered like jewels lined the streets, their fragrance sweet and calming, offering solace to those in need. Great oaks, their trunks thick with age, stood sentinel over the town, their branches heavy with leaves that rustled softly in the breeze.

The sight of so much life was a stark contrast to the devastation that had come before. The earth had healed itself, growing back stronger, as if in defiance of the violence that had ravaged the kingdom.

As they approached the main square, the home of the Lord Ruler of Earth house looming in the distance, the multitude grew thicker. People pressed in closer, and Ros could see the mixture of emotions on their faces—joy, fear, relief, sorrow. A woman reached out, her hand trembling, and Ros instinctively took it. The woman's eyes were wet with tears, but she smiled through them. "Thank you," she whispered, her voice barely audible over the crowd. "Thank you for giving us hope."

Ros squeezed her hand gently, the weight of her responsibility settling heavier on her shoulders. "We'll rebuild together," she promised, though the woman had already been swept back into the mass of people.

Cassian leaned in, his gaze fixed ahead at the looming Earth house. "They look to us for answers. For peace."

"We'll give it to them," Ros said, her voice firm, though inside she wondered how they would ever live up to the expectations of so many. "But not through power or force. Through something better."

As they passed over the stone bridge that crossed the narrow river flowing through Earth house, the towering home of the Lord Ruler now in full view, a burst of petals fluttered down from the trees above, drifting on the wind like confetti. The scent of blooming flowers mixed with the earthy smell of fresh soil. It was as if the land itself was celebrating the return of its rightful guardians.

But Ros couldn't forget the tears, the quiet sobs in the crowd. No victory was complete when so many still suffered.

They had reclaimed Earth house, and now they had a chance to rebuild—something greater than what had existed before. Not just for the highborn or the powerful, but for everyone in Talabrih, from the mages to the magicless. The flowers bloomed in celebration, but the real challenge lay beyond this house.

INSIDE THE HALLS of Earth house, the air was still thick with the aftermath of battle. Ros walked alongside Cassian, her mind already focused on the next step. The war had cost them much, but with Earth house reclaimed, the real work was only beginning.

The vast chamber they entered was bathed in the soft glow of torches. Valeria, Larkin, and Zandor awaited them, standing by a large, rough-hewn table covered in maps and scrolls. The three of them were more than leaders of their people—they were symbols of the old ways, steeped in the traditions of Talabrih, but they were also Rosalinde's best hope for establishing the future she wanted to create.

The tension in the room was palpable as Ros and Cassian approached the table. Valeria studied them with a critical gaze, as if weighing their worth in every step.

"We've won Earth house," Valeria said, her voice smooth but edged. "But this is just the beginning. What's your next move, Ros?"

Ros straightened, meeting her eyes. "Rebuilding," she said firmly. "Not just Earth house, but the entire kingdom. We've been divided for too long, and it's not just the powerful who have paid the price."

Valeria raised an eyebrow, her hand resting lightly on the table. "And what would you suggest? Our people have fought for generations to keep their power. The magicless... they've always served."

Zandor frowned. "You're suggesting they should be our equals?"

Rosalinde's expression hardened. "That's exactly what I'm suggesting. The magicless, the lower castes—they've fought and died in this war too. They've bled for this kingdom, just like everyone else."

Valeria tilted her head, studying Ros carefully. "That's a bold statement. I'm not arguing the truth in your words, but I don't know how others will respond to your vision. Do you truly believe the other houses will accept this?"

Ros stepped forward, her eyes blazing with conviction. "We can't afford not to do this. We've already lost so much, and if we don't change, if we don't offer a future that includes everyone, then there's nothing to stop another uprising, another war. The kingdom can't survive like this."

Larkin frowned, her gaze turning thoughtful. "And what would this future look like? What do you propose?"

Cassian spoke up then, his voice steady and sure. "A kingdom where everyone has a voice. The lower castes, the magicless—they shouldn't be kept at the fringes. We want to establish councils where representatives from all castes and houses can speak. No more decisions made by a few at the top."

"And what of power?" Valeria asked, her eyes narrowing. "You want to share it?"

"Not just share it," Ros said, her voice growing stronger. "We want to build a system where power isn't something that's hoarded by a few. Magic should be used to help everyone, not to control or suppress. We need to reform the laws that bind people to their birthright. The lower castes have skills, knowledge, and strength that we've ignored for too long."

Zandor's voice was soft, tinged with an admiration for the plan Ros was proposing. A smile curled the edges of his mouth. "You speak like an idealist, and honestly, maybe it's time a dreamer was on the throne. But how can we make this happen? What do you expect the high houses to do? Just give up their control?"

Ros crossed her arms, her eyes flashing with determination. "They can either adapt or face another war—one where they'll lose far more than their power."

Valeria stroked her chin, eyes on the map in front of her. "This idea goes against everything we've known. But perhaps it's time. The earth beneath us is always changing, growing, adapting to survive. Perhaps we need to do the same."

Larkin nodded along to whatever she was thinking, as if formulating a plan. "If you can unite the houses behind this vision, if you can offer them something more than just peace—if you can show them a world where they still have influence but also security—then perhaps we can avoid another bloodbath."

Her voice firm, Ros said, "That's what we're offering. A future where we work together to build something stronger, something fairer. But we can't do it without you. Earth house can lead this change. Your mages have power rooted in the land. If you back this plan, the others will follow."

Valeria pursed her lips. "You ask for a great deal. But perhaps..." she said, sighing, "Perhaps we've seen enough death. Enough division."

Zandor asked, "And what if this council fails? What if the magicless and the lower castes rise up and demand more?"

Ros met his gaze, unflinching. "Then we'll face it together. This isn't about avoiding conflict—it's about building something worth fighting for."

Valeria smiled slightly, her sharp eyes gleaming. "I like you, Ros. You've got fire. A rare thing for a Water mage."

"The world is changing," Ros said. "It's time for us to do the same."

"I want to believe in you, truly I do." The Lord Ruler tapped a finger against her chin for a moment, then said, "We'll see if you're enough to reshape the kingdom. I have hope, and it's the first time in a long time that I can say that and mean it. So, Earth house is in. We'll stand behind you while you remake the world."

Ros exhaled, a sense of relief settling over her. This was just the first step, but it was a crucial one. She knew the road ahead would be difficult, filled with resistance and challenges. But she had house allies now—Larkin, Zandor, Valeria, and Florian—and together, they could rebuild Talabrih into something better than it had ever been.

For the first time in what felt like an age, hope flickered in her chest.

Twenty-One

The sprawling halls of Water house felt both familiar and distant to Ros. After the battle for Earth house, returning here carried the weight of their next significant challenge—building the future they had promised. The walls of the estate gleamed in the morning light, the surface of the lakes surrounding it rippling in a gentle breeze. But beneath the calm exterior, a current of urgency ran through the corridors. Mages and servants bustled around the castle, making repairs to what had been damaged and trying to restore a sense of normalcy to Water house. Ros suspected that there may never be a return to the normal they had grown accustomed to.

Ros sat at the head of a long, polished table in the council room, the same room where she'd been planning for war the previous day. Now, it was time for something different—something more lasting. Cassian stood at her right, his arms crossed, eyes fixed on the large map of Talabrih that hung on the wall. Brisa and Elsa were seated nearby, discussing logistics in low tones, while several Shadow-walkers, including Rowan and Sage, waited in the wings, ready to receive their orders.

At the far end of the table, Alaric leaned forward, his fingers tracing the edge of his sword's hilt. His hazel eyes gleamed with the fire of determination, but Ros could sense a shadow of unease in him. He had been a leader of rebels, had used the anger and fury and powerlessness he felt to forge something with a group of people whose main similarities were their pain. Now they were asking him to complete a task even harder than starting a rebellion—building peace.

"Alaric," Ros said, her voice cutting through the low murmurs. "We need you to reach out to the magicless. You know their struggles better than anyone here."

Alaric looked up sharply, meeting her gaze. "I fought for them, yes," he replied. "But it wasn't just me. There were many who led that fight, many who suffered far more than I did."

Ros nodded. "I know. But you have connections with the leaders of the rebellion. They trust you. If we want the magicless to have a voice in this new council, it has to start with them knowing we're serious about including them."

He leaned back in his chair, considering her words. "You're asking me to convince them that the high houses—those they fight against every day just to survive—will now listen to them? It won't be easy."

Cassian stepped forward, his tone calm but resolute. "No one said it would be easy. But we've seen what happens when they're ignored. The rebellions, the bloodshed, the distrust. We can't afford to repeat the past."

"And we can't go on the way it is. The rebels have been instrumental in getting where we are, and now we need to help them take the next step," Ros said.

Alaric's jaw tightened, his fingers tapping against the wood of the table. "I'll go," he said after a long pause. "I'll speak to them, but I can't promise they'll listen. They've been betrayed too many times. It also won't be a good look if I bring back a representative and they arrive at a table full of mages."

Ros looked around the table, around the room. Alaric was indeed the only person there without magic. She'd given no thought when she walked into a room about who would be there and whether she would be in danger just for existing differently than them. Did Alaric have to prepare himself every time he came to her? Did he have to worry that he would be a target because he didn't have magic?

"There will be others without magic," Ros promised. "The last thing I want is a group of people just like me making decisions. Speak to them. Tell them what we're trying to build—a council where every voice is heard. Not just the magic-wielders, but the magicless, the lower castes, everyone."

Alaric nodded, though the weight of the task clearly pressed on him. He stood and turned toward the door. "I'll leave at first light. The rebellion leaders are scattered, but I know where to find a few of them. I'll bring back whoever I can."

"There's a bandit," Ros said. "Her name is Ash. I know little about her, but I want her input for this if you can find her."

"Do you know which house she's from?" Alaric asked.

Ros shook her head. "I met her near Fire house, but that means nothing."

"I'll ask around."

"Thank you."

Alaric stared into Rosalinde's eyes for a long moment before saying, "Anything for you, my queen."

As he made his way out, Cassian watched him go with a furrowed brow. "He'll need allies among them if this is going to work. And even then, the old wounds run deep."

Ros sighed, running a hand through her hair. "That's why we need him. He understands their pain. If anyone can bridge that gap, it's Alaric."

The room fell into a brief silence, the enormity of the task before them settling over the group. Brisa, always the pragmatic one, cleared her throat and shattered the stillness. "In the meantime, we need to organize the council itself. We can't just throw this idea at people without a plan. Who's going to sit on this council? How will they be chosen? What's their role?"

Elsa nodded in agreement. "And it's not just the lower castes and magicless we need to think about. The high houses will resist giving up any of their power. We need to show them that this council benefits them, too."

Cassian crossed his arms, his eyes narrowing in thought. "We'll need a mix of representatives from each house, the lower castes, and the magicless. Each group will need a voice, but we can't let any single faction dominate."

"Which means we need to limit the power of individual houses," Ros said. "We can't let the council be a puppet for the elites. There has to be proper balance."

Brisa began jotting down notes on a piece of parchment. "We can start by drafting a charter—something that outlines the council's purpose, its structure, and the limitations on power. That way, when we present it to the houses, they'll see it as a serious, organized proposal."

Cassian glanced at the map on the wall. "We should also consider the logistics. Where will this council convene? If it's too close to one house's territory, the others might see it as a power grab."

Water house had always been neutral ground, a place where treaties were made and wars were ended. But neutrality didn't mean trust.

Ros looked over at Rowan, who had remained silent throughout the discussion. "Rowan, I want you and the Shadow-walkers to gather information. Find out which houses are likely to resist the hardest. If we know where the opposition will come from, we can address it before it becomes a bigger problem."

Rowan nodded, already mentally calculating how to divide the Shadow-walkers for such a task. "We'll be discreet."

Brisa looked up from her notes. "And what about the

magicless? If Alaric succeeds, we'll need more than just promises. They'll want assurances they won't be pushed aside again."

"We'll give them those assurances, and we'll prove ourselves with our actions," Ros said. "They'll have a seat at the table. Not as a token, but as equals. And when the council is established, we'll make sure their concerns are heard."

As the meeting wore on, they continued to hammer out details—how many representatives each faction would have, how to ensure decisions were fair and balanced, how to avoid the pitfalls of old systems that had failed. But the undercurrent of uncertainty remained. They were trying to build something that had never been done before, something that could either unite the kingdom or tear it apart.

By the time the meeting ended, the room was dim, and the torches cast long shadows on the walls. The plan was far from perfect, but it was a start.

Ros stood by the window, watching the last dregs of sunlight shimmer on the lakes outside. Cassian joined her, his presence steady beside her.

"We've come this far," Cassian said softly. "There's no turning back now."

Ros nodded, her eyes distant as she gazed across the water. "No turning back," she echoed. "But we're not just fighting for a kingdom anymore. We're fighting for something better—for all of them."

"And for ourselves," Cassian added, his voice low but resolute. "This is our future, too."

Ros turned to him, a flicker of determination in her eyes. "Then let's make it one worth fighting for."

THE SUN WAS BEGINNING its descent beyond the rolling hills surrounding Water house, casting a warm orange glow over the lakes and gardens. The day had been long, filled with plans and discussions of the council, but as the evening settled in, there was an unexpected lull—a rare quiet after the storm of battle and preparation.

Ros had sent the others to dinner, knowing they were all famished and tired from the past few weeks. She couldn't seem to steal herself away from the windows. She surveyed the grounds from every room she entered, over-looking her house and the sprawling village beyond as if to make sure it was really there, her thoughts still spinning with all that lay ahead. Alaric had set out to contact the magicless rebellion leaders, and though Ros had offered a Shadow-walker to make the journey faster, Alaric had refused, knowing it would be easier for the rebels to trust him and be open if he was alone. It would be days before they heard any news from him. For now, they could only wait, strategize, and build alliances with the noblemen they hoped to sway.

Cassian entered the room, his presence as grounding as ever. "Everything set for tomorrow?" he asked, referring to the next meeting of their key allies. Earth house was sending Larkin and Lyzandor as ambassadors, and Florian would be there along with a couple of his advisors. Ros expected a productive, yet tiring, planning session with her friends and allies.

She nodded, glancing at him. "We're as ready as we can be. Now we just need the pieces to fall into place."

Suddenly, the heavy wooden doors of the chamber burst open, and a messenger stumbled in, his face pale, his breath coming in frantic gasps.

"Lady Ros, Lord Cassian!" he cried out. "There's been an incident at the gates. You need to come at once."

Ros and Cassian exchanged a look before rushing toward the door, following the messenger through the winding corridors of Water house. As they reached the outer courtyard, the air felt heavy, thick with an energy Ros couldn't quite place.

A small group of guards had gathered near the gate, surrounding a lone figure slumped on the ground. Ros's heart skipped a beat as she recognized the tattered silver and gray robes of Air house. The man lying there, bloodied and barely conscious, was none other than Lord Brensen Cavoll —once a proud and formidable presence, now reduced to a shadow of his former self.

"Help him up," Ros commanded, her voice urgent as she knelt beside him. Cassian was already by her side, carefully lifting Brensen's head as one of the guards handed Ros a canteen of water. She poured a small amount into Brensen's mouth, but his lips barely moved, the water slipping past them.

His eyes fluttered open, and he struggled to speak, his voice raspy and weak. "Ros... Cassian... I tried to make it..."

"Don't speak yet," Cassian urged him gently. "We'll get a Healer. You're safe now."

But Brensen shook his head weakly, a grimace of pain twisting his features. "No time. You don't understand."

Ros leaned in closer, her heart pounding. She tried to pour healing magic into him but nothing happened. She felt the power at her fingertips, felt it trying to move into the fallen mage, but it could not enter his body. She asked, "What happened, Brensen? Who did this to you?"

His breath came in shallow gasps, but he forced himself to speak, each word labored. "It's coming. The villages... gone... no warning..."

Ros's stomach twisted with dread. "What's coming? Who attacked you?"

Brensen's hand trembled as he reached for hers, his grip surprisingly strong despite his fragile state. "Not who," he rasped, his voice growing fainter. "What. We were wrong... we thought Graeme was working with the darkness—"

"Graeme is dead," Ros said.

Brensen grimaced. "It's something else. Something worse than him."

Cassian's expression darkened. "Worse? What do you mean?"

Brensen's eyes flickered with fear, his voice barely audible. "A shadow. It moves through the villages—no army, no magic. Just... destruction. Nothing survives. My men... all gone."

Brensen had told them of something attacking the small villages, of everyone disappearing, but they had thought there would be more time to figure it out.

"Where is it now?" Ros asked, her voice tight with urgency.

Brensen coughed, blood staining his lips. "It's near Earth house. Moving fast. Crossed the mountains and wiped out Winnolds. There's no one left, and no way to stop it. You... you have to warn them. Get everyone out."

"Near Earth house?" Cassian echoed, his brow furrowing. "But we just retook it. We have people there—mages, soldiers. How can we—"

"There's no time," Brensen cut him off, his voice a broken whisper. "It's too late. The villages... gone in hours. It's... it's coming. Hurry. They must flee."

Ros exchanged a glance with Cassian, her mind racing. Earth house was supposed to be a stronghold, a place of safety for their forces and the people. If this thing—this shadow—was nearing, they could lose everything they'd just won.

Brensen's grip on Ros's hand slackened, and his head lolled back as his eyes fluttered shut. The Healer rushed forward, but even before they began their work, Ros knew it was too late. Lord Brensen Cavoll, the proud nobleman of Air house and her friend, had spent his final breath giving her this warning.

A heavy silence fell over the courtyard as the reality of his words sank in.

Cassian rose to his feet, his face hardening with grim determination. "We need to move."

Ros stood, her thoughts racing. "If it's already near Earth house, we don't have much time. We need to evacuate everyone."

"But where will we send them?" Cassian asked, his voice tight with concern. "If this thing is as unstoppable as he said, we can't just keep running."

Ros looked out over the horizon, her mind working through the options. The shadow was something new, something none of them had prepared for. But if they didn't act, Earth house would fall, and with it, any chance they had of holding their ground.

"We'll split the forces," Ros said after a moment, her voice steady despite the fear gnawing at her insides. "Get everyone at Earth house ready to move—soldiers, civilians, all of them. We'll send the mages to try to slow it down, buy us time. Cassian, you'll take a group and lead the evacuation. Take them to Florian."

"Fire house is still being rebuilt. There's not enough room for them there."

"Florian will do everything he can."

"And you?" Cassian asked, his gaze sharp.

"I'll go to Earth house," Ros replied firmly. "We need to know what we're dealing with. I'll bring Brisa and the Shadow-walkers. If we can figure out what this thing is, maybe we can find a way to stop it."

Cassian hesitated, his eyes searching hers. "Ros, this could be suicide."

"I know," she said. "But we can't just run without understanding what we're up against. If we leave Earth house to this thing, it'll keep coming. We have to try."

Cassian sighed, the weight of their responsibility pressing down on him. "Alright. But we do this smart. No unnecessary risks."

Ros nodded, her heart racing. "Agreed."

As they turned to organize their forces, Ros cast one final glance at Brensen's still form, a knot tightening in her chest. Whatever this shadow was, it had to be stopped.

But as she prepared for the mission ahead, she couldn't shake the feeling that they were about to face something far more dangerous than anything they had ever encountered before.

Twenty-Two

The dawn light was barely a glimmer on the horizon when Ros and her companions gathered in the courtyard. The air was thick with tension, the impending threat casting a shadow over the camp. Soldiers moved quickly, securing supplies, preparing for the evacuation. Ros stood at the center of it all, watching as the forces of Talabrih split in two.

Cassian was already in the middle of organizing his group—the largest contingent, composed of soldiers, civilians, and Earth mages who would lead the exodus. They would head east, away from Earth house and the oncoming danger, toward Fire house where they could regroup and hold a defensive position if needed. Larkin and Zandor would accompany them to ensure that they had enough strength to fend off any threats along the way.

Cassian caught Rosalinde's eye from across the courtyard, his expression serious but steady. They had been through so much together, and now they would have to trust each other with their separate tasks. He made his way toward her, weaving through the gathering troops.

"Everything's in place," he said when he reached her. "I've sent Kaith and the other scouts to warn nearby villages and try to find Alaric and the rebels. We'll move out as soon as the first light hits the mountains."

Ros nodded, looking past him toward the soldiers that would follow Cassian. "Are you sure you'll be able to protect them?"

"We have the best chance we can," Cassian replied, his voice calm but resolute. "The Earth mages will hold the ground if it comes to it, and we have enough fighters to keep the civilians safe. But you—"

"I'll be fine," Ros cut him off gently, though her heart pounded with the uncertainty of what was to come. "We will not fight this thing head-on. Just scouting, figuring out what we're dealing with, and if there's any way to stop it."

He studied her face for a moment, worry etched in his eyes. "Don't take unnecessary risks."

Ros smiled faintly. "You sound like me now."

He smirked, then clasped her hand briefly, his grip strong. "Stay alive, Ros."

"I plan to," she replied, her voice firm. "Take care of them, Cas."

With that, Cassian turned and walked back to his group, rallying the last of the soldiers. Ros watched him for a moment longer before turning to her own team. The Shadow-walkers—Brisa, Rowan, Sage, Cressida, Bastian,

Eryx, and Indigo—stood ready nearby, their expressions hard with determination. They would be her eyes and ears as they scouted Earth house for the approaching shadow.

"Alright," Ros called to them. "We head west, split up, and gather information. We need to understand what we're up against before we decide on any action. No heroics—just reconnaissance. If we can find a way to stop it, we will. If not, we regroup and prepare for a defense."

Brisa stepped forward, her usual confidence tinged with a hint of uncertainty. "What if there is no method to halt it?" What do we do then?"

Ros hesitated for only a moment before answering. "If we can't stop it, we'll have to fall back and meet the others at Fire house. But I'm not giving up until we know for sure."

Brisa nodded, though the weight of their mission settled heavily on her shoulders.

The first rays of sunlight broke over the distant mountains, signaling the time to move. Cassian's forces began their march east, disappearing over the hills as Ros and her group mounted some horses loaned to her from the Earth house stable. They turned west, toward the unknown threat that loomed over them.

The ride was silent, the tension palpable. The beautiful landscape of Talabrih felt strangely still, as if the land itself was holding its breath in anticipation. Past Earth house were thick forests and rolling hills, fields of flowers and gardens that their people prepared for the harvest. Though the country was more lovely with each passing mile, the air grew colder, and an unnatural heaviness settled over them.

By the time they were a few miles out from the village of Winnolds that Brensen had said was destroyed, the sun was high above, but the light felt muted, as though the very sky had darkened. Ros stopped atop a hill overlooking the village. From there, she could see nothing but the spire of the worship house in the center of town, the tallest building in the tiny village. The rest of the village appeared hazy, lost to a fog that would not clear. The air was thick with an eerie stillness. No movement. No sound. Not even the rustle of leaves as an animal passed in the nearby woods. It was as if the land had gone silent.

"There's nothing left," Rowan murmured, his sharp eyes scanning the horizon.

Ros's stomach churned as she followed his gaze. What-ever had passed through here had left no one behind.

"We need to move closer," Ros said, her voice steady despite the fear that gnawed at her.

The group descended the hill in silence, approaching with caution. As they neared the village, the full scope of the situation became clear. The place was deserted, their homes and shops still standing and no sign of a battle, but as empty as if no one had ever lived there.. No bodies. No signs of life—or death.

"It's like they just... disappeared," Cressida muttered, her voice barely audible.

Rosalinde's heart hammered in her chest as they reached the outer perimeter of Winnolds. Whatever had struck seemed to have stopped at the edge of the town and had not continued further yet, leaving a stark difference between the brilliant beauty outside the village and the eerily quiet inside, where once vibrant gardens were wilted and lifeless.

"What could have done this?" Indigo muttered, her hand resting on the hilt of her sword.

"I don't know," Ros replied, her voice tight. "But we need answers."

Ros took a step forward as if she planned to enter the village proper, but Brisa put a hand on her shoulder, stopping her short.

"We won't find anything out here," Ros said.

Brisa shook her head. "My people aren't going in there. And neither are you."

Ros pursed her lips. "Like it or not, I'm your queen."

"I know, and I like it, actually," Brisa said, hands on her hips. "And I will do whatever it takes to keep you safe. Even if that means safe from you, because you can't control yourself. You will not be the Martyr Queen on my watch."

Ros opened her mouth to object but stopped suddenly, her breath catching as she caught sight of something at the far end of the courtyard—a figure, barely visible in the dim light. It moved slowly, almost aimlessly, as if lost.

"Do you see that?" she asked, motioning to the others.

Brisa squinted, her eyes narrowing. "Is that... a person?"

Ros didn't respond. She took a cautious step forward, her hand on her sword. The figure continued to linger, but as they neared, its shape became clearer. It wasn't a person —it was a shadow, formless and shifting, its edges blurring with the darkening air around it.

"What in the name of the elements..." Bastian breathed, his voice full of disbelief.

Ros's heart raced as the shadow seemed to pulse, its darkness growing, expanding toward them as soon as it recognized their presence.

"Back up!" she shouted, drawing her sword as the shadow surged forward, faster than anything she had ever seen.

They scattered, barely avoiding the tendrils of darkness that lashed out like living whips. Ros felt the cold bite of the shadow as it brushed past her, sapping the warmth from the air around them.

"We can't fight this!" Brisa shouted, her eyes wide with terror.

Ros gritted her teeth, her sword glowing faintly as she summoned what magic she had. "Fall back! Now!"

They turned and ran, the shadow closing in behind them like a living storm.

Ros and her group sprinted away from Winnolds, the shadow swirling as it followed their path. Every step seemed heavier, the air thick with the oppressive presence of the entity chasing them. Her mind raced with possibilities, none of them promising.

"My magic isn't working!" Bastian shouted, his voice echoing as they rushed into the protection of the trees.

Ros glanced back, her pulse quickening as the formless darkness surged closer. "We can't outrun it forever. Maybe if we can put some distance between us and... that... we can use our magic."

The thing chasing them had reached the forest's edge now. As soon as it touched the trees, they withered right in front of Ros and the Shadow-walkers. Everything that came into contact with it suddenly looked abandoned.

"Over there," Brisa called.

She pointed into the near distance where ruins jutted from the earth like the bones of a forgotten giant; weathered stone pillars stood in uneven rows, half-sunken into the ground as though the land itself had tried to swallow them. Each pillar bore intricate carvings, their once-sharp details now softened by the passage of time, eroded by wind and rain until they were little more than faint impressions of an ancient language no one alive could read. Vines snaked up their sides, clinging to the rough stone, as though nature had claimed these relics as her own. The air around the ruins was thick with a strange, heavy silence, as if the pillars themselves held secrets too old to be spoken aloud. As the darkness chased them over the land, shadows pooled between the pillars, giving the place a haunting beauty—an eerie reminder of a world that once was, and a warning of what could come again.

But the shadows did not cross into the circle the pillars created.

"Hurry!" Rowan yelled. "It can't cross the barrier."

They darted into the protection of the columns, panting as they pressed against the cold stone, listening for the eerie sound—or rather, the lack of sound—of the shadow.

Ros leaned back against the pillar, trying to catch her breath. "It's like nothing I've ever seen before," she said, the gravity of their situation finally sinking in. "How can we stop something that doesn't seem to have form?"

"We've fought armies, mages, and monsters, but this..." Rowan shook his head, his face pale. "It drains the very life from everything it touches."

Indigo clenched her fists, his usual confidence shaken. "We need a plan. We can't keep running."

Ros nodded, her mind racing. "We'll have to figure out a way to trap it, contain it somehow."

"How? It's massive," Bastian said.

Ros squinted, looking around. The thing fully surrounded them now, blocking out the sky and the forest entirely. Despite the nearly all-encompassing nature of the shadow, it still couldn't enter the ruins. "We don't know enough about it yet. There's something here, something we're missing."

A low, almost imperceptible rumble vibrated through the ground beneath them, pulling their attention to the perimeter. The shadow coiled and undulated on the invisible barrier, like smoke climbing a pane of glass.

"It's waiting," Sage muttered, her voice barely above a whisper.

"Why?" Ros asked, narrowing her eyes as she watched the shadow's erratic movements. "Why hasn't it attacked yet?"

"I think it's feeding," Cressida said, her voice tense. "The destruction in the villages... it's been consuming something. The earth, the life around it—draining it."

Ros's breath caught. "It's not just feeding on magic— it's feeding on the land itself."

The realization hit her like a blow. This entity wasn't just a mindless force. It was something far more dangerous, something ancient, feeding on the very essence of Talabrih. And it would not stop until it had consumed everything.

Ros exchanged a glance with Brisa. "If it's draining the earth, the only way we can fight it is to starve it."

"How do we do that?" Eryx asked, his voice tight with frustration. "We can't exactly cut off the land."

Ros's eyes flickered toward the shadow. "Maybe not, but we can trap it in a place where it can't feed. Somewhere where it's cut off from the land and the magic."

Bastian frowned, his brow furrowing in thought. "Where would that be? Everything around here is connected to the land."

Ros nodded slowly. "We'll need the Earth mages for this. If they can create a barrier strong enough—something that severs the connection between this thing and the land —it might weaken it."

Brisa's eyes widened in realization. "If we can disrupt the flow of that magic around this entity..."

"We starve it," Ros finished, her voice firm. "But we'll need to act fast."

Rowan said, "We don't have much time. Whatever this thing is, it's gaining strength."

Ros stood, her mind racing as she formulated a plan. "We need to get back to the Earth mages. Larkin, Zandor, Valeria—they'll know what to do. We'll have to lure this thing into a place where the mages can create the barrier."

"But how do we get back to them if our magic is unusable near it?" Cressida asked, her voice laced with fear.

Ros took a deep breath. "We'll have to bait it. It's drawn to life, to magic, right? We give it what it wants."

Brisa's expression darkened. "You're not seriously suggesting someone goes into that thing? Night mages might be known for our destructive personalities and foolish decision-making abilities, but we're not actually trying to die."

Ros shook her head. "I wouldn't ask any of you to do that."

They sat in silence for a moment before Brisa said, "Because you're going to do it."

Ros nodded.

"No," Rowan said. "We can't let you."

"You're not letting me. You can't stop me."

"The hell we can't," Cressida said.

"I'm not facing Cassian after you go walking through that mess," Eryx said.

"We wouldn't survive," Indigo said. "He would end us."

Ros pressed her lips into a tight smile. "Cassian isn't here. But I am, and I'm your queen. I appreciate your loyalty to him, but my heart belongs to the people of Talabrih, to my kingdom. And I have to fix this. To try, at least. While he is leading Earth house to safety, it is up to me to figure out how to fight this thing. I can't do that from here."

"You can't do it if you're dead," Brisa said.

Sage said, "And your magic isn't working to shield. Even if you could, it might not help."

"If I could direct it," Ros said, fingering the fire bracelet Ombretta had given her, "where could we take it?"

"The ridge north of Earth house. It's barren, mostly rock and cliffs. The Earth mages could create a barrier there," Indigo said.

Ros nodded, her decision made. "That's where we'll take it. I will pull it off of you. Use your magic as soon as you can. Find the Earth mages and tell them the plan. We'll draw it to the valley, and the Earth mages will cut it off."

"There's nothing we can do to stop you?" Bastian asked.

Ros smiled grimly. "This might be our best chance; honestly, it may be our only chance."

"Let's hope you're right," Sage added, her tone grave.

"I would just like to offer my protest again before you do this," Rowan said. "We have a few minutes of reprieve here in the Earth Cradle; if you could wait a little longer, we could sort it out."

The Earth Cradle. Ros looked around, surprised to

realize that she had, in fact, been there only days before. Days for her, at least. For her friends in Faerie, it was barely more than a single day. Had Ombretta even begun her mission to rescue her brothers, or was she still getting reacquainted with Faerie? With the Earth Cradle still providing a ring of protection for them, Ombretta likely hadn't found Faolan. For all Ros knew, Strahn could have had Ombretta arrested as soon as she arrived.

Ros took a deep breath and cleared away the thoughts of her friends in Faerie. She couldn't help them. She wasn't sure she could help the people sitting beside her even now. Though, in thinking about them, she came up with an idea.

"If I disappear into the shadows and you see no change, I need you to do me a favor," she said.

Brisa's eyes went wide. "Queen Rosalinde, I implore you. If there's a possibility this won't work, do as Rowan suggested and pause long enough to think this through. Let us help you find a solution."

"The longer we wait, the less likely we'll be safe here."

Ros met eyes with each of the Shadow-walkers and, with a deep breath, told them of her time in Faerie. She explained what had transpired with her new friends, including the soon-coming attempts to free the Princes. She did, however, leave out that Ombretta was fae and on her way to save her family. That wasn't her secret to share.

"So, you're saying this place, the only place where we're safe from this shadow, could disappear at any moment if an imprisoned fae prince gets loose?" Rowan asked skeptically.

"That's where you went after you were abducted from Earth house?" Brisa asked.

Ros nodded. "I know it sounds too wild to be real, but I swear to you that every word is true. I need you to understand and believe me, because if I can't lead the shadow away, the fae might be your only hope."

Brisa nodded, her face solemn. "What do we do?"

Ros opened her mouth to speak, but had the sudden impression that the Shadow-walkers weren't the only ones listening. She held up a hand to the group as she surveyed the shadows surrounding them. She saw nothing but darkness, anything but—

There.

Barely perceptible in the distance, Ros could make out a shape. It slithered and coalesced into a humanoid form, but as soon as it realized she was staring into the space it occupied, the shadow dispersed as if it was never there.

A chill went up her spine. She said, "It's watching us, listening."

"Why would it want to know—"

Ros hushed Bastian before he could form the question. "Maybe this isn't the only land it wants to destroy. If it could find its way between the barrier that connects each world, the devastation would be unthinkable."

They sat in silence, the weight of the situation growing heavier with each passing minute. Finally, Eryx said, "If you're really going to do this, you'll have to risk it."

"If the shadows absorb you as it seems to have done everyone else, it may have the knowledge anyway," Indigo said.

"Very comforting," Sage muttered.

"We don't know if that's really how it works," Cressida said.

"You're right," Indigo said. "It could be much worse."

Rowan said, "Ignore them and call on your friend. You said it may take a while to answer, anyway. Reach out to them quietly, so the shadows cannot retrieve the information from your words. Even if you do not get lost in the darkness, we may still need the help of the fae."

"You're right," Ros said.

She closed her eyes and reached into her memories, bringing up every beautiful thing she could recall about Datura Whimsy. The Moonchild shared a connection with her after all they had been through, and even though their ties had been released, she knew they would still feel it if she called on them. As quietly as she could, she whispered Whimsy's name into the still air around them.

Ros opened her eyes and looked around. She wasn't exactly expecting Whimsy to suddenly be there, but they certainly would have been a welcome sight if they were. After another moment, Ros said, "I've done all I can do from here. It's time to try the main part of my plan."

The shadow was still lurking in the distance, watching them as though it could sense their every move. Ros's heart pounded, but there was no turning back now. She advanced toward the edge of the ring and held her hand up between the stones. The darkness swirled violently in response, as if it was desperate to reach her.

Ros turned and looked over her shoulder. "If I don't make it—"

"You will," Brisa cut in.

"If I don't," Ros repeated, "tell Cassian I'm sorry. Tell him I tried. Tell him I loved him."

Ros inhaled a deep breath, thought of fire, and watched as the bracelet on her wrist lit up. It wasn't like her regular magic, wasn't tied to the same power source. It blazed against the darkness beyond. With a release of her breath, and the boldest step Ros had ever taken, she walked past the stone and into the waiting shadows.

Afterword

Thank you for reading *The Flame of Fire House*. I hope you enjoyed the continuation of Rosalinde's adventure! If you did, please leave me a review, stop by my website, or find me on social media. I'd love to hear from you. You all mean the world to me and I'm truly thankful for the time you've given my book.

If you'd like to try another story with royals, magic, and new book boyfriends, check out my mermaid series starting with *Black Sea Bright Song*.

You may also like my sci-fi series under Shelly Jarvis: The Book of the Golden One duology starts with *The Dreamwalker* or the 3-book post apocalyptic series Little Star begins with City of Trials.

About the Author

Michelle Jarvis is a fantasy romance author with a penchant for royalty. She loves diverse characters and believes everyone deserves a love story.

While Michelle has had her own love affair with writing since she was in elementary school, it wasn't until her thirties that she realized how much fun it was to turn up those romantic subplots. Now she's combining her love of fantasy and her newfound passion for romance to put them into the hands of readers.

Michelle lives in West Virginia with her partner and their rescue dogs–Gimli, Gus-Gus/Gooser/Goosie-boy, Bones, and Fergus.

For free books, bonus scenes, and news about upcoming releases, sign up for Michelle's mailing list on her website: www.authormichelle.com

Also by Michelle Jarvis

City of Trials

"Lady *Mad Max* meets LGBTQ+ *Hunger Games*"

The Dreamwalker

"*Space Harry Potter*"

Black Sea Bright Song

"*The Little Mermaid* if it was told from Ursula's point of view"

Writing for Weirdos: How to Craft Compelling Short Fiction